HOW TO BE A
SISSY MAID

HOW TO BE A
SISSY MAID

JO SANTANA

First published in Great Britain by Miro Books

ISBN 978-1-906320-09-6

Printed and bound in the UK & US

A catalogue record of this book is available from the British Library

Cover design by Miro Books

CONTENTS

FOREWORD

Becoming a sissy maid to a deserving mistress is one of the most exciting and satisfying lifestyles a man can adopt. Although not for everyone, many men and women will derive immense satisfaction and erotic sensations from this kind of activity.

To dress up in all of the frilly, feminine finery of the sissy maid takes a bold person indeed. To be laced into a rigid corset and practice walking on high heeled shoes requires patience and determination. Equally, for the mistress to encourage and train her maid into these lifestyle choices is just as difficult for many. Yet the rewards are incredible. A feeling of deep, erotic satisfaction and the knowledge that one's partner is completely and totally trusting of the other, is itself a big reward. And the sex!

The title 'sissy maid' describes the humiliation aspect of mistress and sissy maid fun. It is just that, to humiliate. It does not describe the real personality of the sissy maid, neither does the mistress need to be viewed as a leather clad iron studded dominatrix with whips and chains. The whole object is to put aside reality and spend some time in harmless, warm fantasy, a fantasy that is togetherness between two people.

Do you feel called to serve? Your mistress needs you, so talk to her about helping you become her maid. You will find it the most exciting and erotic activity you have ever undertaken.

JO SANTANA

CHAPTER 1

The Mistress and the Sissy Maid - what kind of people are they?

A simple introduction to this book is that there is no such thing as a typical mistress and sissy maid. Of course, conventionally (if that being conventional is at all possible in this the topsy turvy world of the sissy maid) it involves a partnership of a man and a woman. They can be married or unmarried. They can be partners or not. In certain situations, the sissy may pay a 'professional lady' to help him enact the role of a sissy.

In conventional relationships involving a man and a woman, the sissy is a man that cross-dresses and adopts ultra feminine behaviour, engaging in typical female activities (e.g. housekeeping, putting on make-up). A sissy will typically assume the submissive role to dominant partners. Sissies can also identify with other fetishes and sexual practices such as: erotic humiliation, bondage, petticoating, cuckoldry, chastity, leather, latex/pvc, infantilism, corporal punishment, etc.

As a lifestyle desire or fetish activity a sissy's feminisation tends to be a voluntary transformation from male to female, either physically, behaviourally or both. Generally this is temporary for the period of the role play, although sometimes it can be permanent in nature. It is also normally conducted in private, although again, in the anything goes world off sissy maids, often the sissification can be more public.

People who identify as a sissy represent a wide variety of sexual orientation and to the type of feminine dress and appearance they prefer. A sissy might be, and often is, a heterosexual and only desires to be dominated by a woman, while the homosexual sissy might desire to be dominated by a man. And in forced feminisation gender-play, a heterosexual sissy might have the desire to be forced by his female partner to engage in sexual acts with a man. The important part of being a sissy maid, of course, is the uniform, the classic maid's uniform, or French maid's uniform, the more frills the better.

Most heterosexual sissies act out their feminisation desires almost entirely online and/or in the privacy of their homes.

Sissy maid training is the most common of these themes. In a typical scenario a male submissive, or sissy maid, is dressed in the sexy and frilly maid uniform to help enhance the sexual thrill. The activities the sissy is made to perform range from mundane household tasks that a real maid would perform, to degrading tasks that invoke erotic humiliation. The sissy maid might also be instructed to perform sexual acts, however these acts usually place the sissy in a submissive or passive role.

So what qualities are we looking for in the dominant side of the mistress and sissy maid relationship, the mistress herself? Does she have to be the leather clad, high booted, studded, whip wielding femme of sexual cartoon imagery? Certainly not! Unless of course this is what she wants, and what both partners in the relationship agree to. But many mistresses are plain housewives, partners, girlfriends or occasionally casual friends. They have one thing in common, that is that they wish to give their male partner, the sissy maid, the experience they want, in return for getting their own quid-pro-quo. What does the dominant get out of the deal? Again, they get what they want and decide in partnership with the submissive, with the sissy maid. Note that in partnership is the important phrase and the important factor will be consent.

Consent is a vital element in all sexual play, and can be granted in many ways. A written form may be used, or a simple verbal commitment may be enough for others. Consent can be limited both in duration and content. It's not unusual to grant consent only for an hour or for an evening.

When play lasts for more than a few hours, it's a good idea to draft a contract that defines what will happen and who is responsible for what. Work out what both parties want in advance, and set out the limits.

For long term consent, a slave or maid contract may be used. These kinds of contracts are only an agreement between consenting people and are usually not legally binding, of course. As far as we are aware, true slavery is in fact illegal all parts of the world! Thank goodness. These contracts are simply a way of defining the nature and limits of the relationship.

After a contract is made, some partners celebrate the event with a ceremony, in which perhaps the sissy maid will be dressed in their full uniform ready to begin work. Some ceremonies become quite elaborate and can be more involved. It's all up to you and your imagination.

Can the dominant part of the relationship, the

mistress, retain her femininity whilst her (normally male) partner is attired in all of their full, frilly, corseted and high heeled glory as a humble maid? Of course she can. We often associate dominant women with whips, chains and a pitiful man grovelling at their feet while licking a pair of vinyl boots, but you may be surprised to learn that dominance doesn't always translate into sadism. On the contrary, many dominant women play the superior role in relationships simply because their man simply wants them to adopt this role. The female may indeed be strong-willed, feisty and independent, but this doesn't mean she wants to be a leather goddess.

If the role playing means that she is to adopt the part of the mistress, she should be able to do this in the most feminine of ways. After all she is in charge, if she wants her sissy to act the role of lady's maid that is for her to decide and insist upon. Having decided how she wishes to play her role, she needs to begin dominating her sissy, moulding them to her will. Note that proper eye contact is extremely important when it comes to asserting dominance. A truly dominant mistress can influence a sissy maid with the subtlest of glances. Most sissy maids, when faced with a mistress' stern glance, turn to jelly and happily let her do whatever she pleases.

We see therefore that the mistress/sissy maid

set up is a type of sexual relationship where the female takes the non-traditional dominant role and the male is the submissive. This is often known as 'Femdom', short for female domination. The female is often referred to as mistress, dominatrix or goddess. Femdom can be a lifestyle or just play in the bedroom. There are numerous activities that are considered female domination. As we have said, the limits to this kind of play are all in your imagination.

The mistress/sissy maid relationship can extend beyond the private play within one's own home. Lifestyle femdom is usually where a relationship extends beyond bedroom play, it can involve public humiliation, fetish events known as public outings.

Much of the mistress/maid sexual play can involve spanking, bondage, CBT, foot fetish, body worship, golden showers and other pain or humiliation activities often seen in BDSM scene. Even anal submission via strap-on dildo is by no means uncommon. Other femdom includes sexual denial of male satisfaction and focus on the sexual satisfaction of the woman. It can be achieved through male chastity to keep the sissy maid obedient and eager for the relief while he is attentive to his mistresses needs.

"Tendency to inflict and receive pain during

sex is the most common and important of all perversions."

Sigmund Freud

It is a fact that there are a great number of men for whom becoming a submissive, a sissy maid, is a form of stress relief and is important for their mental well being. There are many instances of female domination covered in mainstream media where the professional dominatrix is usually wearing leather clothes and high heel boots. Successful business men are known to visit professional highly paid mistresses to get their relief.

It is important for the mistress to realise that different sissy maids require different skills and abilities from their mistress. For the mistress it is often difficult for her to perform the act of domination in a way that is both convincing and will satisfy the maid. She needs to be able to present herself and act in such a way that the sissy maid can both feel comfortable giving up control to her and also feel her taking over. Some women try to be successful mistresses but cannot carry it off properly, that is, in a way that satisfies their sissy maid. They may appear caricatured instead of in command, for example. So the technique of being a successful mistress may not come naturally, but will need to be learned. Remember, all those mistresses out there, the rewards are great. Your own willing maid ready to do all of the housework, keep the house immaculate, work long hours into the evening doing the ironing and ready to satisfy you sexually at any time you wish it.

Good acting skills and imagination are important for the mistress to learn, where the sissy maid requires fantasy support to enable them to get the greatest satisfaction from their 'work'. These are not skills that require emotional understanding of the sissy maid. They just require a little imagination and determination. Perhaps in the early days, a suspension of belief will help too.

Mistresses must generally be capable and interested in sustaining an emotionally or spiritually intimate relationship with the sissy maid in the long-term. This allows the deep trust to develop which is required for the maid's surrender, at least within the act of performing her duties, to give both the maid and their mistress the great pleasure and satisfaction that is the huge reward for performing this kind of role play. Because the sissy maid experiences a need, and not simply a desire, the mistress must be more responsible and recognise her duty to the maid to satisfy that need.

It is important for the mistress to give her maid step by step rules. You need to tell them things like they are not allowed to do unless you give them permission, their bedtimes and so on. They want to have you take control of their everyday life and give them rules to live by. This is the emotional make up of the sissy maid, as a mistress you have everything to gain by giving them what they want. In so doing, you will certainly get what you want, generally many times over.

Television shows reflect real life, at least sometimes. Nowadays it is very common for women to be in control, in and out of bed. It is because they are more independent and at times even earn more than their men. That at least is part of the reason. Most men adore their woman being in control. At least, those men inclined to the sissy maid lifestyle. Remember, when a couple is involved in a power exchange relationship such as domination and submission, or mistress and sissy maid, there is an assumption that the dominant partner is the one who is in control. After all, a submissive in a relationship is seeking a partner in which they can give their control up to and a dominant is looking for a partner whom she may control.

This assumption, however, is misleading. The submissive is making decisions throughout the relationship. Their first decision is to actually enter into such a relationship with a person. They are not forced into the relationship. They make a conscious decision, based on the information they have been given by the other person, as to if the relationship will meet their needs. The next decision that the sissy maid makes is in regard to boundaries. In a good relationship boundaries need to be discussed in the beginning. Both the mistress and the maid have limits as to how far they will go in a relationship, certain areas in which they are not willing to explore. Some areas may be taboo, and the couple makes an agreement to not explore such areas. This could be anything from knife play to heavy bondage or even sharing with other partners.

It is very important for the sissy maid to lay out their boundaries in the very beginning of the relationship. This way the mistress can make an informed decision as to if they want to continue in the relationship. It is also important for the mistress to express their boundaries. If a mistress' favourite scene involves strap on dildos and anal sex, and the sissy has that listed as an absolute no in their list of boundaries, then the relationship will obviously not work.

Another reason why it is important for the sissy maid to express what their boundaries are in the beginning is so the mistress will have a feel for what she is working with. She is not going to want to have to second guess every scene wondering if the maid is going to get upset and refuse to submit. That would defeat the purpose of the exchange process. Once boundaries have been set, the sissy maid gives their mistress permission to control them within those boundaries.

To sum up this chapter, being a mistress or sissy maid is something that is open entirely to the imaginations of the participants. Because of the discrete and sexual nature of this kind of role-play, it is not one you are likely to see happening in your street. Behind the net curtains, however, it will be a different story. There will be more than a few people nearby having fun in this way. Use your imagination, set limits and consents and go for it. Mistresses, draw up your list of chores, decide how you would like to be sexually pleasured. Maids, get a maid's uniform, the frillier the better, put on the rubber gloves and get down to work. It is a role-playing game where all parties stand to gain a great deal, and there is no downside.

CHAPTER 2

What kinds of duties does the maid perform?

The sissy maid will be required to serve in a variety of roles, as house maid, lady's maid, cook, cleaner and anything else the mistress decides she requires her maid to perform. In addition, she will invariably be required to fulfil a sexual role in the bedroom, serving her mistress in any way that she desires.

Firstly, as a housemaid, the sissy maid will be required to keep the whole house immaculately clean. Secondly, as a lady's maid, the sissy will be required to attend to every personal need their mistress may have, dressing them, helping with their hair and makeup, ensuring that their clothes are carefully laid out each morning. Thirdly, of course, as a sex object, the sissy maid is firmly under control of the mistress. They must make certain that they carry out whatever duties the mistress may want to satisfy her sexually. More of that later.

Some sissy maids live in chastity. It is their mistress who decides if and when she is to get any sexual release. The sissy maid's sexuality is diverted into service. Their sexuality is no longer about personal gratification, it is transferred into loving obedience and service instead. This can be incredibly rewarding for both the sissy maid and the mistress. The longer they are kept in chastity the more submissive and obedient they become. Their whole world becomes about pleasing their mistress.

Here is a typical sample of a cleaning session, a necessary part of the sissy maid's duties, normally performed at the start of the day.

As a sissy maid, the first step is to don a pair of rubber gloves. Then thoroughly clean the bathroom making sure to remove any hair that is lying around, this ensures that hair doesn't interfere with any of the cleaning you do later. Then spray a mould remover all through the shower recess. Leave that while it does its work and clean the toilet. Make sure the lid, the seat, under the seat and the bowl, are all scrubbed clean. Flush the toilet and wipe down the seat. Then get to work on the bath and sink with a cream cleanser. Use an old toothbrush to clean under the base of the taps to clean out any grime that has lodged there. After wiping down, rinse off with hot water. This ensures there are no streak marks left. Return to the shower recess. Wipe down the mould remover and use the toothbrush to get into any nooks and crannies that cannot be reached with your sponge. Again rinse off leaving no streak marks. Next use a paper towel and a window cleaning product to clean the mirror. It is vital this is done perfectly as the mistress will be looking in that mirror at herself. With a bucket and mop clean the floor and allow it to dry before replacing any mats etc.

The proper care of delicate lingerie, whether it's your own or your mistress', is vital. It is best to soak lingerie in cold soapy water and never mix dark colours with whites or light colours. Using your finger tips only, gently agitate each piece and make sure your fingernails are filed nicely to avoid snagging and damaging the fabric especially if it's lace or silk. Rinse each piece separately in cool water and very gently wring out excess water. Never squeeze lingerie like a dish cloth. Instead fold a large fluffy bath towel in half lengthwise and place the lingerie carefully on it then gently roll it up and press down lightly to remove most of the water. Hang your mistress' bras and panties or whatever else you washed on the shower curtain to dry. When dry it's time to neatly fold and put them away. Taking proper care of your mistress' lingerie and other fine clothes will go a long way in pleasing her and making her happy to have you serve as her maid. Always remember it is a privilege to serve as a maid, doing a good job using your own initiative has rewards.

A large part of the duties of the sissy maid include taking the role of the lady's maid and this requires a unique set of skills. The lady's maid is a personal servant responsible for the lady of the household. Duties include the care of the wardrobe and mistress' private rooms, and care, cleaning, pressing and mending of mistress' clothes, preparation of clothes for packing and so on.

Lady's maid's typical skills include the following:-

- Knowledge of care of all fabrics, and leather.
- Ability to hand wash delicate items like silk and cashmere.
- Sewing skills for minor repairs and alterations.
- Knowledge of cosmetics, makeup and other personal grooming items.
- Knowledge of hair care and styling.

For the really dedicated sissy maid, here is a formal

description of the part of a lady's maid, taken from a bygone age. You can adapt it to suit your fantasy, taking as much or as little as you wish out of this piece:

'A lady's maid attends to her mistress' appearance. She arranges her hair and assists in dressing her. She packs and unpacks the mistress when travelling. She may also make her mistress' dresses. Depending on the size of the household, she may assume some of the housekeeper's duties. In a typical day, she brings up hot water as necessary, brings up tea before breakfast, prepares clothes for dressing, assists the mistress in dressing, puts the room in order, puts out necessities for walking, riding or driving, assists in taking off her outdoor attire, puts evening dress in order, assists in dressing her for dinner, sits up for her, assists in undressing her, puts away her jewels, keeps her wardrobe in repair and washes the lace and fine linens. She also attends to any pets the mistress may have.

Morning Duties

- You will wake at six o'clock.
- Before the Mistress rises, you should put away any clothes from the evening before and prepare what she is to wear that morning.
- At the appropriate time you must wake the

Mistress of the house by bringing her tea and thin slices of bread and butter, a newspaper and any correspondence. You should run her bath, help her to dress and do her hair.

- While the Mistress takes her breakfast, you must tidy the personal effects in her bedroom and arrange outdoor clothes if she is leaving the house.

- Throughout the day you must be ready to run any errands your mistress requires.

- After breakfast, if the Mistress intends to go out, you will need to assist her to change into her outdoor attire. If she wishes it, it is customary for you to accompany the Mistress if she is going out.

- At eleven o'clock tea you may take tea in your maid's quarters, you may take lunch when the Mistress allows.

Afternoon Duties

- After dinner, providing your Mistress does not require your service, you may choose to busy yourself with needlework or repairs to the Mistress' clothing, or wash her underwear and personal garments.

- Providing you have the consent of your Mistress, you may take your leisure between half-past three and four o'clock.

- You should tidy the Mistress bedroom once again, and begin to prepare her clothing should she wish to go out, possibly for dinner.

- From half-past six onwards you should make yourself available to assist the Mistress as she sees fit. The Mistress should always be the focus of your attentions.

- The remaining part of the evening is to be spent at your leisure, until the Mistress retires to bed when

> you will need to assist her undressing and loosen and brush her hair.'

Wow, that will certainly keep the sissy maid from getting bored. As we said, you can choose as much as little out of this list to do. The choice is yours, or more properly the mistress', to make. The sissy maid can be a lady's maid, a laundry maid, a house maid, in fact any kind of maid that the participants desire. And, of course, a sex maid, the sissy maid will be always available to give the mistress whatever, sexual gratification she desires.

Let's look at an actual scenario, we ask a real-life mistress:

What qualities are you looking for in a sissy maid?

For a sissy maid, I am looking for a man who works and in fact lives to please me. If they take no joy in being my maid there is really no point in them being involved in the first place. They should be attractive, immaculately groomed, particularly with regard to their uniform, their hair and makeup, shoes, underwear, everything should be perfect. They should be in good health and emotionally stable. My sissy maid needs to be attentive, have a great memory for detail, a strong sense of humour and be able to cope with whatever comes their way.

When did you realise that you wanted to adopt the role of mistress to a sissy maid?

I became really accepting of the dominant side of my personality throughout a journey of introspection and self-examination that I have undertaken in the past few years. I realised that I wasn't getting something that I wanted and needed out of my relationships. In order to be happy I was going to have to look at how I was approaching gender issues. I found that dominant men were no fun to be with. They tended to be selfish, immature, and that each connection had made me progressively more miserable.

Thinking back on the happier experiences I realised these were situations where I took on a dominant role and my boyfriends had in fact been of service to me and had served me as submissive. Although in the early days, men with the commitment and strength to be maids were few and far between. I recall feeling comfortable, safe, loved and secure with these men knowing that my needs were seen to and I was able to take a position of greater power and femininity, which made them happy as well. Taking it into consideration and taking it all apart, I saw that to be happy I was going to have to engage within the context of a female-led relationship, and that I wasn't going to be happy with a man who didn't want to serve me, latterly in the role of maid.

What common mistakes do submissive men you have met make?

My real dislike is for sissies to be vulgar, obscene or to send me disturbing emails or phone messages or photographs. I don't like it when they are unable to conduct a platonic and pressure-free first meeting, when they show up dressed badly, in poor taste or look like a tramp. I like them to pay for the first date, but not to talk back. They should be reliable and punctual and during conversation, never answer my questions with a question.

I want my sissy maid to be sweet to me, saying something nice about how I look. I do not want them to fish for compliments about how good they look. I especially don't want them displaying a sense of guilt or shame over their own submissive nature. They should not start any conversations about sexuality without waiting for me to bring it up first. They should also give me my personal space or trying to create a false sense of intimacy.

There you have it. If you are a female, you will understand that your wants and desires are totally normal, the same as most other females in every part of the world. You are a normal healthy girl, with normal healthy appetites. All you are looking for that your partner is the same, with the essential difference, of course, that they will be the submissive, your very own sissy maid.

For the sissy maid, you can see what is expected of you in the relationship. To always be sensitive to what your mistress requires and put your own self interest on the back burner. To be smart and neatly turned out, a maid to be proud of, and never, ever, ashamed of your submissive role. The result can only be a very happy and fulfilled relationship. Bring together the right dominant and the right submissive, the right mistress and the right sissy maid, and you have a relationship that will be more rewarding than you ever would have believed possible.

We started out by looking at the typical duties of a sissy maid. We have given examples of how it used to be done, in the heyday of the lady's maid, or housemaid. We have shown what kind of sissy maid the average mistress would expect to make the partnership happy and fulfilled. We have shown the aspiring mistress that what she would expect from her maid is pretty normal.

A sex slave? No.

She wants a loving partner, in or out of bed. One who is kind, considerate and hard working, albeit in the uniform of a Victorian or French maid, depending on their preference. But above all she expects, rightly, a sissy maid who puts her first every time. There you have the recipe for the perfect relationship.

CHAPTER 3

The Rules of the Game

When we talk of rules for mistresses and their sissy maids, these come into two separate categories.

Firstly, of course, the mistress will have rules of conduct for the maid to follow, to make sure that they comport themselves to the mistresses satisfaction. These include how the maid should conduct themselves with regard to behaviour, dress, makeup, hair, and of course punishments that may be applied if the maid fails to keep up these standards.

Secondly, there are consensual rules. This is a game of domination and submission, to be enjoyed, to enhance the lives of the participants. If this is to be successful, the mistress and maid need to agree limits so that each knows that the game will not go beyond what each of them wishes.

Thirdly, there will be the rules that apply to the daily list of chores including times for the maid to work, which tasks they should carry out and times for breaks and meals. For the relationship to be successful these need to be adhered to, and they need to have a list of punishments should the maid not satisfy the mistress that they have kept to the rules.

Rules of Conduct for Sissy Maids:

- When being spoken to, stand still, keeping your hands still and always look at your mistress or the person speaking.

- Never let your voice be heard by the mistress, unless they have spoken directly to you a question or statement which requires a response, at which time, speak as little as possible.

- In the presence of your mistress, never speak to another person unless only for necessity, and then as little and quietly as you are able.

- Whenever possible, items that have been dropped, such as spectacles or handkerchiefs, and other small items, should be returned to their owners on a tray.

- Always respond when you have received an order with a curtsy, and always use the proper address: "Mistress", "Ma'am", "Miss" or "Mrs," as the case may be.

- Never offer your opinion to your mistress.

- Always "give room": that is, if you encounter your mistress in the house or on the stairs, you are to make yourself as invisible as possible, turning yourself toward the wall and averting your eyes.

- Except in reply to a salutation offered, never say "good morning" or "good night" to your mistress.

- If you are required to walk with your mistress in order to carry packages, or for any other reason, always keep a few paces back.

- You are expected to be punctual to your own place at your mealtimes.

- You shall not receive any visitor or friend into the house, nor shall you introduce any person into the house, without the consent of your mistress.

Consensual Rules for Sissy Maids and their Mistresses

It is very important to set limits for the mistress and the maid to follow.

- Agree on the number of hours and days each week that the maid should work.

- Agree on whether or not the maid should be exposed to the public or not.

- Agree on punishments, how far they should go.

- Agree on a 'Safe' word. A word that can be used so that if things are going too far, they can be stopped by saying this word.

- Agree on standards of dress and duties, so that neither feels that either too much or too little is being done or demanded by either side.

Daily and weekly Chores.

This is simple, in the light of the agreement on hours

and days worked, the mistress must decide what tasks she requires done, and what she reasonably can expect her sissy maid to complete. It is of course for her to decide. The sissy maid's only duty is carry out their mistress' wishes. In the event that the work proves to be impossible, or far too arduous, there should be room for discussion, and of course there is always the safe word that can be used if the maid feels that things have gone too far.

The mistress should draw up a schedule for their maid, perhaps this can be pinned up so that the sissy maid always knows what is expected of them.

Punishments

Here is an account of how one mistress we spoke to applies punishment to her sissy maid when she does not perform to her satisfaction. This is corporal punishment, we will look at other forms of punishment later.

> "I am firmly convinced that an unruly or naughty maid deserves the humiliation and pain of a sound chastisement. Let us say that you are incensed with the careless work of your maid. Very well, you cane or birch them. When my maid is to be punished they are sent to a room and told to put on a kind of hood which hides their head and shoulders. In that way, the mistress does not have to look

at the impertinent maid while she is applying punishment, and of course the sissy maid will feel the punishment all the more, prevented by the hood from seeing when each blow is about to fall."

I did ask whether her maid was submissive enough to be expected to go alone into a room knowing they were to be punished and to prepare all alone.

"Oh, yes," she smiled at this, "because when we made our agreement between mistress and maid, I informed them of my methods. They were given ten minutes. If the maid has not complied with my requirements, they are informed that they will be either removed from their post as my sissy maid, or they will be sentenced to another whipping at some future time. In that latter event, they are told they will be punished with twice the count they were to have had and will then be put to work doing the most menial tasks. In nearly a year since I allowed my sissy maid to start work only once have they refused punishment. They later broke down and humbly apologised to me a few days later and asked for their whippings."

While we were interviewing this particular mistress, she called in her sissy maid.

"In fifteen minutes you will go to the punishment room at the back of the house."

She explained that when the maid is sent to the punishment room she is expected to put on the hood, hold up their skirt and remove their knickers and be kneeling on the couch facing the door. The mistress may apply any correction or position she may choose. Obedience is understood. If the maid you are to whip argues or refuses to obey, you apply four extra strokes.

The hood was of thick black cotton, covering the maid's head entirely, with slits for nose and mouth but none for the eyes; it covered the throat as well. The maid knelt facing her, naked from the waist to their stocking tops. The mistress told the maid she was to receive ten strokes of the whip for her transgressions. At this point the maid thanked her mistress for correcting them, as they had been taught to do. The maid certainly flinched and squirmed as the whip was applied, and small noises of pain came from inside the hood. Afterwards, the sissy thanked their mistress and was made to stay kneeling with their knickers down for a further twenty minutes and reflect on their poor performance.

Here is a more extensive list of punishments, choose as few or as many as you wish, provided of course that it is all consensual. Remember the safe word if things get out of hand.

Give the sissy maid one or more nasty chores to carry out. This can include things such as extra cleaning of the cooker, ditto windows, scrubbing the floor with a nail brush. Tasks assigned as punishments should not include tasks that are part of the sissy maid's normal duties.

Make the sissy maid sleep on the floor, or in some other uncomfortable place.

Instruct the maid to stand in a corner for a given length of time. This will give them time to think about what they have done wrong. The length of time can vary from few minutes to an hour or more. It is suggested that the mistress try this punishment for themself, to get a sense of how difficult this punishment may or may not be for the length of time in question.

Make the sissy maid write out long piece or essay, perhaps even lines, that describe what they have done and how they will make sure that they correct their behaviour in the future.

Make the sissy maid kneel for a long period, preferably on a hard surface. This can be very uncomfortable and will certainly make your maid think twice before they misbehave in the future. This punishment can be carried out with other enhancements, such as manacles, a blindfold or hood, possibly a gag, although be very careful to monitor this at all times for safety reasons.

Kneeling on a hard surface can be made more severe by dropping a handful of uncooked rice on the floor where the maid is going to kneel. Once the time period is done the sissy can be instructed to clean up the rice as part of bringing the punishment to a close. This is another punishment where it is suggested the mistress try it to get a feel of the punishment. The same cautions and time limits apply to this as when kneeling without the rice. The mistress should also be aware that the rice sometimes causes marking of the skin.

Keep the sissy maid on a restricted diet. Obviously some common sense is required with using food restrictions a punishment. Being sent to bed without dinner is a certainly not going to cause a healthy individual any harm. However, be careful not to take this to extremes, especially where health issues may be concerned. Does the sissy maid like the occasional glass of alcoholic beverage? Cutting this out for a period can be a useful punishment.

Restrict access to those leisure activities that the maid enjoys, computer games, watching TV etc. The restriction can be total, where the sissy maid is not allowed any access to the items, or it can be limited to a certain amount of time. There is a wide range of options under this heading.

A cold shower works well as a punishment. It is important to define the length of the shower. Less than five minutes is generally quite safe for any fit person. Experiment with this until you feel you have a happy balance.

Make the maid spend time in the corner of a room by themselves, so that they can calm down and think about what they have done wrong. This is often a good choice when the mistress wants to avoid adding stress to a situation.

Being restricted to home can be a relatively effective and low stress punishment. External factors greatly affect the harshness of being restricted to home. This means that the same punishment is more or less severe depending on what else is going on in the maid's life at the time. Being restricted when one has already bought tickets to go out to the theatre is more significant than being restricted when one has no plans.

Speech restrictions can range from requiring the maid to speak in third person to requiring them not to speak at all for a period of time. When silence is used as a punishment it is helpful to have the maid carry around a notebook and pen so they can convey necessary information. Requiring a maid to speak in third person is an effective way to make her aware of self-cantered behaviour. Many times a sissy may not be aware of how just often they refer to their own opinions and desires in casual speech.

Apologising in a public forum stresses humility. The mistress must carefully consider the reaction of those who are going to hear the apology.

If the mistress controls the finances in the relationship restricting spending money can be used as a punishment. This is same as a parent withholding allowance and generally works best over shorter terms such as a week to a month. When it becomes longer than a month the punishment starts to become the norm.

Lastly, here is a slice of discipline straight from the pages of a 19th century fashion book.

Remember the hobble skirt, which occasionally make a re-appearance in modern clothing? Hobbling is not excessively mentioned in the pages of sissy maid training, or even BDSM manuals. It comes from the hobble skirt of Victorian England. The skirt was so narrow at the ankles that the maid, or woman wearing it, could barely hobble. By shortening the maid's steps the hobble skirt makes them feel very helpless and trapped, perhaps as importantly it stops any chance that they could run away.

It makes the sissy maid's steps much more feminine, they will carry themselves more like a lady, especially if they are also wearing a tight, preferably whale boned corset and high heeled shoes. It is likely that this arrangement will give the maid an ultra feminine 'sway' to their walk, so that they look especially feminine and sexy and they go about doing the housework.

The basic hobble skirt is very easy to make or to get hold of, available from shops, mail order or even charity shops if you are lucky. A good hobble skirt can be made from a twelve to fourteen inch chain attached to the inside of a long skirt, so that outwardly it looks like a normal skirt, but actually it can tightly hobble the wearer. It would be best to forbid your sissy maid to climb stairs in a hobble skirt.

Yet another device from the days of the Victorians is a backboard, a classic Victorian invention, apparently used to correct the posture of generations of young women. It consisted of a padded wooden board with straps at shoulders and waist to hold the back rigidly erect and prevent the shoulders from drooping.

It is entirely possible to make one of these backboards yourself. Cut a piece of thin wood to the length of your maid's torso from their shoulders to the tops of their thighs, slightly wider than the shoulders at the top and narrowing to the width of the hips. Pad it well with firm foam rubber and cover with a soft, absorbent material. Velvet is ideal, but a there are many other materials that can be used to cover the board. You should attach narrow vertical straps at the shoulders to hold the arm firmly to the backboard.

There is no reason why you should not instruct your sissy maid to make the backboard themselves. Thus, they are the architect of their own punishment.

Remember, with all of these rules and punishments, everyone will have limits, and all of these limits will be different. Observe those limits and always remember the safe word.

CHAPTER 4

What to Wear - The Sissy Wardrobe

Here is where the sissy maid can really go to town, if necessary literally, to deck themselves out in the uniform that is their heart's desire. Depending on what type of maid you wish to be, you may consider a different sort of uniform for different occasions, say for cleaning work a simple classic black dress and white apron, with cap. For serving your mistress her meals, perhaps you might consider a satin uniform. Many sissy maids love a satin uniform more than any other in their wardrobe. However, these should not take your attention away from the daily uniforms, Victorian uniforms and other styles.

Remember to begin by allocating wardrobe or

cupboard space, so that your uniforms can be hung up neatly and be kept ready to use at all times. A creased uniform is embarrassing to both you and your mistress. If you need to keep your uniforms hidden away, buy a trunk or suitcase in and keep it accessible, using a combination lock. Remember to press it regularly or it will get untidy and creased and impossible to wear at a moment's notice.

The first part of your uniform to buy is your maid's dress. Some dresses come as complete sets, others don't. Even if your uniform does come with an apron, you may want to consider getting another, smarter, perhaps frillier affair. Black or pastel dresses cut in variations on traditional styles, with short or long skirts are correct attire. A uniform should look well cut and well made, not like a reject from a Chinese fancy dress wholesaler.

The uniform is a badge of submission. Dressing in a proper domestic uniform proclaims to everyone and to the maid themselves that they are a servant who is at the service of her mistress. They are dressed like a domestic servant because that is what they are. They are 'in service' as a domestic maid servant. The uniform has much the same effect on a maid as the harness does on a guide dog for the blind. While still in their male clothes they will act in a typically male fashion but once put into their uniform their behaviour changes and they become a docile hard working maid servant.

The mistress normally will choose, or at least approve, the maid's uniform. Some mistresses allow their maid to choose their own uniform, but this is best avoided if possible. The mistress is in control, not the maid. Many sissy maids choose a short, frilly black and white French maid's outfit, together with frilly knickers and a little petticoat, wholly impractical for scrubbing floors. Since a sissy maid is basically for domestic work, it is a domestic uniform she wears more often than not. Other uniforms can be chosen for waiting at table or serving at a party.

When on duty the sissy maid is not allowed to appear outside the maid's bedroom in anything other than their full uniform. They are not allowed to wander about the house without their cap or apron or wearing some other dress. This rule will be especially important for sissy maids who have a strong cross dressing streak in them and who have a collection of dresses. The temptation to dress glamorously will be strong. A mistress will need to be firm about this rule.

Uniforms must be practical. While looking menial and smart, a uniform must be practical. A maid needs to be comfortable and well protected from soapy water. There is not much point in asking them to scrub the kitchen floor on their hands and knees wearing a frilly white apron. It will soon be a mess no matter how hard the maid tries to keep it clean. The waterproof plastic or rubber apron is essential. Something a sissy maid can slip on and off easily as required. A maid who is properly dressed will not have to worry about keeping their dress clean and will be able to concentrate on their scrubbing or washing up.

The apron signifies the menial status of the sissy maid. Large white cotton bib aprons for domestic work. A large waterproof apron will be needed when working in the kitchen or when washing floors and windows etc. A pretty frilly bib apron is suitable for evening wear.

A matching cap completes the uniform. The cap can match either the apron or the dress.

The sissy maid must be taught to take great care of their uniform. It will need to be frequently laundered and starched so that they look very smart. A sissy maid ought to wear their uniform with pride. A mistress will be ever vigilant to make sure her girl is properly dressed and looks trim. No mistress wants a dirty untidy girl about her house. A sissy maid should be taught to check her appearance in the mirror. She may have to straighten her cap or the bib of her apron. She should always do this before entering the presence of the mistress.

If the sissy maid has a full head of hair then she

can have it cut short and set in tiny curls. A head of tight little curls looks pretty and keeps the hair out of the face while they are working. A sissy maid who is balding will obviously have to wear a wig. It must be practical and will be comfortable to work in as well as looking attractive.

High heels must not be allowed for domestic work. The sissy maid must wear white flat shoes for general works and flat, black and comfortable shoes for evening wear and serving at table on formal occasions.

For a new sissy maid stockings are essential, black or navy blue. They must be thick so as to endure kneeling on floors while scrubbing.

Knickers have an arousing effect on many men. A sissy maid into a pair of bloomers or directoire knickers is right. They are practical, hard wearing and not sexually arousing.

A long line bra helps keep the artificial padded bust in place. A sissy maid should look like a good strong country girl who has just arrived in service.

Sissy maids must report to their mistress at the end of their day's work. They shows their schedule and reports on their progress. If the mistress has the time will carry out a tour of inspection, running her fingers along surfaces looking for dust and checking the rooms she has asked to be spring cleaned. If the work is not up to standard the maid is sent back upstairs to put on her cleaning uniform and report back to the mistress to finish the cleaning left undone. This may seem harsh but it soon gets a sissy maid working to a proper standard. If a mistress is lenient early on and settles for low standards of housework then she will find it hard to insist on the highest standards later on. Don't forget that the advantage of having a sissy maid is that she is able to impose a high standard of work and discipline. Something that isn't usually possible with a daily char.

A mistress must remember that sissy maids are only human and will need to be encouraged as well as corrected. The inspection is often the opportunity for the mistress to give her sissy maid a little pep talk. At the beginning of the day the mistress can encourage the maid by telling them that she is looking for a high standard of work and she is relying on them to get on with her work efficiently and quietly as there is a busy day ahead. If at the end of the day if the work has been well done then the mistress should speak words of praise and encouragement. Even if there have been lapses, the good mistress will find things to praise as well as expressing her displeasure. The mistress always explains that her reprimands are only for the maid's own welfare and well being. Both mistress and sissy maid want to reach a high standard. A good sissy maid will feel guilty at having let their mistress down, rather than feel resentful at being told off or scolded.

It has great importance the way a sissy maid behaves, and how the maid dresses. Here is an account of one sissy maid getting into uniform, to give you an idea:

'The maid's classic, black French maid's dress was displayed on a hanger, its lines forming the shape of a demure but shapely woman even as it hung there empty. While the uniform was classic, it was far from ordinary, made with very high quality and an exaggerated femininity rarely seen outside the movies. Short flared skirt, dramatic puffed sleeves and white lace trimming every conceivable edge. The maid took it off the hanger, unzipped it, put it on the floor and stepped in, pulling it up and doing up the zip. It fit snugly, and intentionally so. The short skirt flared out in all directions, the square collar was edged in flounces of lace. They couldn't help but turn a bit and watch the skirt billow. Turning to the dresser they saw a pile of lace and ornaments, and a strange black item. Realising what it was the dress was pulled off and the maid squeezed into a tight, black corset, which would give an ideal feminine shape.
They had difficulty in tightening it and had to

beg the mistress for help, but with each pull on the strings at the back they felt excited   Their shape was changing and felt like they were becoming a new person. When it was finally on and the strings tied round, the waist was compressed by nearly four inches which forced them to take short, quick breaths. The new maid pulled a roomy pair of directoire knickers up, the silky garment reaching down to their knees. Then they pulled on their camisole, which was fastened shut with hooks and eyes and finally more lacing. Next came the petticoats, a waist petticoat first and then a full length petticoat which reached down past the knees Once the dress was back on, they pulled on their maids apron, a voluminous white cotton frill garment that almost entirely covered the dress. Next the shoes, ankle length boots with three inch heels, laced on to the feet. Then it was accessory time. They put one thing on after another, bracelets, earrings, a necklace, a watch pinned to the frilly apron. They fastened their hair flat to the head with a hairnet and clips and pulled on and adjusted a wig which was already styled into a Victorian effect complete with bun. Finally, a cap was fastened over the wig, finishing the outfit in a flurry of white lace and ribbons. When this was completed, the maid went to the mirror to put on make up. This was a long and painstaking affair with lipsticks, foundation, mascara and a range

*of feminine accessories. The maid checked
their appearance in the mirror. It was perfect,
mistress would be satisfied.'*

Certainly the most important of these garments
for the maid to wear is the corset. It is the device
that underpins the maid's feminine shape, as well
as the prison that holds them in bondage to their
mistress. Mistresses and maids will differ in the
severity of what they consider becoming to the sissy
maid, and a number of suggestions are therefore
put forward so that the maid may have some idea
of what might be expected of them under a routine
of corset discipline. The standard of dress already
described represents the basic way of life for the
sissy maid, and it will be modified to suit the tastes
and convenience of mistress or maid, domestic,
financial and social circumstances. Here is a
description of one lucky sissy maids corset training
A light regime requires rigid foundations and
complementary underwear when the maid is on duty,
or if required by the mistress, even when the maid
if off duty but in their own home. As a minimum,
the maid should be tight laced into a traditional
corset on at least one day a week and a use firm
elastic foundation with more decorative underwear
at other times if the more tightly laced corset is too
much to bear. However, the maid must always be

laced in for at least one full day each week. When in the house, on or off duty, they should preferably be made to wear camisole, knickers and petticoats and may never be without stockings!

Even when an easier regime allows for elasticated foundations or any but the most modest underwear, it is really better when the maid is put into a traditional corset on one or two days a week or perhaps once weekly and for one whole week each month.

A strict regime is based on daily lacing-in, and a shorter traditional corset would normally be worn. A long discipline corset is worn for a day or two at regular intervals. Underwear will make fewer concessions for weather and uniforms should be long dresses of a Victorian or Edwardian style. Sleepwear includes a liberty bodice and night stockings, modesty knickers, nightdress and night bonnet.

Once a routine has become established, mistresses and maids will seldom be faced with any serious problems of discipline. However, while being trained to a suitable standard of service, the maid usually attempts to rebel. Where strict standards are being aimed at there may be the temptation to begin training on a lighter, more liberal regime, but this can be a mistake. While there may have to be some concessions to allow for the unfamiliar harshness of a traditional corset, it is best to begin as you intend to continue.

Of the problems that arise, resentment of corsetry and underclothing are the most frequent. Hot weather in particular brings pleas to change into lighter garments and even to leave essential items off. Concessions for hot weather should be made only with caution and in order to avoid clothing being inadequate when it becomes cooler. Foundations are never reduced to allow for hot weather, and only petticoat, vest and knickers may be changed from heavy materials to light materials or cotton. Reduce underwear sparingly and only one garment at a time. The maid can be both stubborn and cunning, and supervision may be called for if there has been the opportunity to slip off a vest or roll stockings down. A favourite occasion for rebellion is tight-lacing, and all but the least spirited will attempt to loosen their stays if discovery can be avoided. There will be pleas to moderate lacing-in or even to postpone a tight-lacing day. Here too, concessions are a mistake.

Days for being laced into the traditional discipline corset must be set in advance and adhered to without fail. Until they can be trusted to do it for themselves, the maid must be laced in by the mistress, and the remainder of their dressing will also have to be supervised. With the corset lace tied in a double bow at the back, all the proper underwear and a uniform dress that fits snugly at the waist and fastens at the back, disobedient relaxation of lacing will be too laborious to escape detection. Once compliance in these matters has been established, the subject might be left to lace themselves in, though results will always be better if the lace is pulled in from the back by strong, determined hands. The rigid corselette or corset and brassiere worn on other days must also be properly fastened to control the figure and deportment.

It has been said that it is impossible to understand how a sissy's mind works. This is not true of all sissy maids. The attitude of some to being laced in is a case in point. At first there is defiance, then rebellion, then sullen acceptance. In the end they willingly lace themselves in, but still with voiced complaints and sometimes tears. They always resent being corseted, yet eventually under strict guidance seem to welcome the daily ordeal and day-long constriction so eagerly that one might even have to suggest they loosen their stays when the inevitable headache or faintness occurs. They loathe their corsets, they are constantly in rebellion at the restraints of bones and busks and lacings, yet would not venture more than a few feet from their beds without them.

However, long and relentless training will be needed

before this inexplicable state is reached, and few sissy maids have the good fortune of a mistress with the severity and determination to establish lacing-in as an every-day habit. The important feature in corset discipline is a regular, predetermined regime enforced with unbending ruthlessness the mistress. The maid may not simply decide to wear a milder corset or fewer underclothes as they please.

Remember, the life of the sissy maid is one of submission. The corset is a major and important part of that submission, the wearing of which will be an enjoyable part of the mistress and sissy maid ritual once the maid has been properly trained and disciplined in its use.

CHAPTER 5

Hair Removal

If we are to be a maid to make our mistress proud of us, we need to look our best. There are some who manage to look like a lorry driver in drag. Other maids go to a great deal of time and trouble to look very feminine and alluring. It is this kind of appearance that we hope you will aspire to, So we begin with the first stage of preparation, removal of masculine hair so that your skin looks soft, smooth and so feminine!

Hair removal can be of two types, either permanent or temporary. Some maids may use a combination of techniques, using permanent hair removal in places where they do not wish their increasingly feminised appearance to be too obvious, and temporary hair removal where, for example, they may need to go into the office on Monday and a more male appearance is required.

All people have hair follicles on most of the surface of their skin. The number of hair follicles in men and women is similar. The differences in the appearance of hair between men and women lie in the hair type. A hair follicle can produce a fine, thin, light (lacking pigment) hair that is almost invisible. This is called vellus hair. In contrast, other hair follicles may produce a long, thick, dark hair that is readily visible to the eye. That type of hair is called terminal hair.

Epilation is a technique whereby the hair is removed by its root. However, not all epilation techniques will also destroy the active cells at the hair root. Depending on the particular type of epilation method, the hair may be eliminated temporarily or permanently. Electrolysis, for example, is a method of epilation that aims to eliminate hair permanently. On the other hand, plucking the hair (using wax or tweezers) is a method of epilation where the hair is only removed temporarily.

Depilation is a method of hair removal that does not involve the root of the hair, but a region higher up the hair shaft, at or near the surface of the skin. Examples of depilation are shaving and the use of depilatory creams. All depilation methods remove hair only temporarily.

Shaving is fast, simple, convenient, and painless. Many maids use this method for shaving their legs and armpits as well as, of course, the face.

Note: The myth that shaving the hair increases the rate of growth and produces thicker hair is without foundation. The upper part of the hair that is found above the surface of the skin does not contain any living material. This upper part is composed of lifeless keratinous tissue and therefore cutting or shaving it cannot result in the growth of coarse, thick, dark hair, and does not encourage hair growth. When a hair (which as stated, is merely dead keratinous material) is cut, there is no effect on the hair root where the active cells that cause the hair to grow are found. The mistaken impression arose, perhaps, because the short hairs (stubble) that are seen on the skin after hair is shaved are straight, prickly, and relatively thick compared with their length. As the hair grows longer, it loses its prickliness.

Shaving, being not painful, quick and safe, can be used over wide areas of skin and on any type of skin and any hair—fair or dark. The main disadvantage of shaving is that the hair grows back relatively soon after and has to be re-shaved. Also, skin may be nicked and there may be skin irritation.

Bacterial infection in the shaved area may occur. These infections (medically termed as folliculitis) tend to occur more frequently in the groin. To prevent cuts, skin irritation, and infections, it is advisable to use a new, sharp blade; to soften the skin by wetting the area to be shaved and covering it with a liberal layer of lather; and to shave as gently as possible, with minimal pressure of the blade on the skin.

In cases where the skin tends to be injured, each stroke of the blade should be directed toward a new area of hair, and a stroke of only a few millimetres should be used each time—this is preferable to trying to cover wide areas of skin in one movement. In this situation, once the hair has been soaked in water and lather, the excess lather should be removed so that the precise location of the short hairs, and their direction of growth, can be seen in order that they can be shaved correctly.

Another method, equivalent to shaving, is mechanical scraping. In its classic form this is done using a pumice stone. As with shaving, this procedure needs to be repeated every few days. Vigorous scraping, which may result in redness and irritation of the skin, should be avoided. A similar technique is to rub the skin gently in a circular motion with a depilatoric glove, whose surface is composed of fine sandpaper. An antiseptic alcohol solution should be applied before scraping the skin. Following the scraping, moisturisers containing soothing preparations (such as aloe vera or witch hazel) should be applied.

In shaving, the hair is cut off at the skin surface, at the level of the dead keratinous component of the hair. Therefore, there is no effect on processes that occur in the live region of the hair root. On the other hand, if the maid employs plucking the hair root is actively pulled out, and the consequences are unpredictable and change from person to person.

Repeated plucking can cause some damage to the hair root. In most cases, plucking has no effect on the shape or structure of the hair (for example, many women pluck their eyebrows without this causing coarse, dark, thick hair to grow back). However, the reaction of the eyebrow hair to plucking is unpredictable, differing from one person to another. Sometimes plucked hair follicles of the eyebrows tend to grow hairs that turn in different directions, deviating from the natural direction of the eyebrow hair. Relatively more commonly, following repeated plucking, the hair tends to become finer and thinner. Note that in the area of the eyebrows, after plucking (or repeated plucking), the hair may not grow back. Often the recovery period following the plucking of eyebrow hair is relatively long, and may last for more than a year. Therefore, unnecessary plucking in this area should be avoided. It should be noted that many people who succumbed to fashion trends of the past are now forced to draw-in their eyebrows because the eyebrow hair has thinned out owing to repeated plucking.

Sometimes there is the impression that, following plucking, the hair becomes thicker and coarser. In most cases, that appearance is not a result of the plucking, but rather a reflection of the normal life cycle of the hair. A hair follicle that is plucked while it is in the resting phase will later be in the active phase, with new hair growing from it. The new hair grows and because it is in the active anagen phase, it can look thick, dark and coarse. However, this is merely a reflection of the particular phase of the hair's life cycle at that time, and is not related to the plucking.

Plucking can be done using tweezers, thread, warm or cold wax or warm melted sugar, and special instruments. There may be pain, which some people cannot tolerate. Inflammation of the hair follicles may also occur. This is caused by microscopic injuries during plucking and subsequent infection by bacteria. It is also possible that scars may develop in the areas of plucked hair.

As opposed to shaving, the smooth, hairless skin

left behind after plucking remains that way for a longer time. The hair tends not to grow back for a few weeks in areas that have been plucked. Plucking with tweezers or a thread is used where there is a small number of hairs to be removed (such as the eyebrows, chin, etc.), or where there are isolated hairs in some part of the body (for example, around the nipples). The thread is coiled around the hair and allows it to be plucked out easily and efficiently.

Using wax to remove hair is, in fact, a form of plucking that can be done over relatively large areas of skin. The wax that is used is obtained from beehives.

The treatment is performed as follows:

The wax is heated until it melts and smeared over the area where the hairs are about to be removed. The wax solidifies within a minute and the hairs become stuck to the wax and trapped in it. The layer of solid wax can then be peeled away rapidly from the skin, pulling away the hair trapped within it. Using wax detaches hairs from the skin near the root— deeper than the effect of shaving, which removes the hair at the skin surface—so the effect lasts longer than with shaving. It takes a few weeks for plucked hairs to reappear above the surface of the skin. A few days after using wax, new hairs may appear. This is not re-growth of the plucked hairs, but growth of new hair that happened to be in the active growth phase of its life cycle. These hairs were due to appear in that area regardless of the wax treatment.

Wax is only partly effective, since it cannot trap and hence cannot remove short hairs that have just reached the surface of the skin; hairs of less than 2mm in length are usually not caught up in the wax.

Irritation or allergic reactions may occur, ranging from mild irritation, manifested by transient redness and slight stinging, to moderate and severe reactions. If there is merely a mild skin irritation, it is sufficient to apply soothing preparations (such as 1% hydrocortisone cream or aloe vera preparations) on the affected skin. In the case of more severe reactions, the patient should be referred to a dermatologist. Inflammation of the hair follicles may appear following waxing. It is manifested by the appearance of many small, red lesions, or by the presence of many small lesions containing pus, where the hairs grow. In this case, the patient must be referred to a dermatologist. The technique may be painful, people feel the pain to different degrees.

Careless use of hot wax may burn the skin.

Waxing may cause the appearance of superficial small blood vessels on the skin. In most people who have used wax for years, specific or significant problems don't occur. There have been reports that after prolonged use of wax there is less re-growth of hair, and the hair that does re-grow tends to be finer and thinner. Theoretically that is possible, because repeatedly plucking out of a hair by the root does damage the root. Nevertheless, most women who use wax find that they have to continue treatment time after time, for years.

To use, warm wax, thoroughly clean and dry the skin. Some people recommend sprinkling a light layer of talc on the skin to absorb any residual moisture or oil, so the wax will stick better to the skin. When using warm wax, make sure that it is not too hot by testing a drop on the back of the hand. Never use wax on injured or diseased skin. There is no point in advising wax treatment for someone who has recently shaved the area or used a chemical depilatory agent, since the hair in the area will be too short and will not become stuck in the wax. In such a case, wait two or three weeks until the hair has grown longer.

Smear the wax on the skin in the direction of the hair growth.

Wait a few minutes for it to cool and harden, and remove it by peeling if off against the direction of the hair growth. Following the treatment, it is advisable to disinfect the skin with alcohol.,

Warm melted sugar is not popular, because it is painful. The technique is based on applying warm, melted sugar, which is sticky, then pulling it off together with the hairs that have stuck to it. A strip of material is used to help pull out those hairs that have stuck to the sugar. The method is similar to warm wax treatment.

Cold wax works the same way as warm wax. The hair is trapped in the cold wax, which is then quickly peeled off, thus plucking out the trapped hair. To be precise, the correct chemical term for cold wax is in fact not wax at all, but a mixture of various sugars. Usually these preparations also contain citric acid. This combination of compounds produces a thick and sticky substance, which is generally quite effective in pulling out hairs. In general, the stickier the substance, the easier it is to remove the hair and the less painful it is.

Instruments on the market for plucking hair are based on the action of a spiral spring. The hair is caught up in the spring and pulled out. The pros and cons of this technique are the same as those for plucking hair in general, but the design of these instruments allows hair to be removed quickly from larger areas, such as on the limbs.

Preparations are usually marketed as creams or ointments, but some are also available as gels or foams or in a roll-on form. Chemical depilatories contain substances that dissolve the keratin fibres from which the external part of the hair is made. The hair comes off at or just below skin level. The hairs tend to break in the places where the keratin is slightly deficient or unevenly distributed. Hair comes away at the skin surface when treated with depilatory cream. Chemical depilatories affect only the external part of the hair and not the living root. Therefore, within a few days the hairs growing back can be noticed.

Instructions for Using Depilatory Agents

- Follow the manufacturer's directions carefully. The instructions may vary depending on the type and concentration of the preparation.

- Do not leave the preparation on the skin for longer than is specified in the instructions.

- Do not apply to the face a cream meant for the legs.

- Do not use these creams on damaged skin. In any case of skin disease, a dermatologist should be consulted.

- The first time a preparation is used it should be tried on a small area of skin, usually the arm, to confirm there is no abnormal sensitivity to the substance. Evaluation of the test area should be done after 24 to 48 hours. If, after that trial application, there is no skin irritation (redness, swelling, itching, or burning sensation), the substance can be used over wider areas of skin.

- Clean and dry the skin thoroughly before using the depilatory agent.

- The skin adjacent to the area to be treated can be protected by covering it with a fatty preparation, such as petroleum jelly.
- After leaving the depilatory agent on for the required time, wash it off with lukewarm water.

The main advantage of using depilatory agents is that they, as opposed to other methods, are painless. There are, however, possible problems.

- There may be skin irritation. Chemical depilatories may affect not only the hairs but also the superficial layers of the skin. This irritation is due to the fact that both the hair and the skin are composed of keratin. The degree and extent of irritation depend on the type of preparation and its concentration. Mild irritation may be treated by application of 1% hydrocortisone cream or aloe vera preparations. In more severe cases, the person should be referred to a physician.
- They can give rise to an unpleasant odour.
- Re-growth of the hair can occur following the use of a depilatory agent. Although the hair is removed at a deeper level than with shaving, within a few days, the hairs growing back can be noticed.

This is another method of dealing with the problem of excess hair. It is intended for women with a fair complexion who wish to camouflage hair on the face and arms. The hair is still there, but is less obvious and almost invisible. A bleaching preparation can be made by mixing hydrogen peroxide with ammonia in a low concentration. The effect of the solution contain substances that dissolve the keratin fibres from which the external part of the hair is made. The hair comes off at or just below skin level. The hairs tend to break in the places where the keratin is slightly deficient or unevenly distributed. Hair comes away at the skin surface when treated with depilatory cream. Chemical depilatories affect only the external part of the hair and not the living root. Therefore, within a few days the hairs growing back can be noticed.

Instructions for Using Depilatory Agents

- Follow the manufacturer's directions carefully. The instructions may vary depending on the type and concentration of the preparation.

- Do not leave the preparation on the skin for longer than is specified in the instructions.

- Do not apply to the face a cream meant for the legs.

- Do not use these creams on damaged skin. In any case of skin disease, a dermatologist should be consulted.

- The first time a preparation is used it should be tried on a small area of skin, usually the arm, to confirm there is no abnormal sensitivity to the substance. Evaluation of the test area should be done after 24 to 48 hours. If, after that trial application, there is no skin irritation (redness, swelling, itching, or burning sensation), the substance can be used over wider areas of skin.

- Clean and dry the skin thoroughly before using the depilatory agent.

HOW TO BE A SISSY MAID

CHAPTER 6

How the Maid should Conduct Themselves as a Female

To be a successful sissy maid, one to make your mistress proud of you, you need to look like a real woman. That means taking care with every aspect of your body, your hair, nails, skin, makeup, dress, deportment, the way you speak and even, dare we say the way you think. Thankfully, once you are corseted and uniformed, ready to do your mistress' bidding, much of this will come naturally. It is hard to be aggressive and macho when wearing a tight corset, long dress and apron, layers of frilly underwear, make up and wig and high heeled shoes. Very hard, in fact!

Here are some suggestions to make your sissy

quest more possible and successful.

There is one detail that can quickly give away that fact that you aren't as girlish as you seem, this is the hands. Men have bigger hands than their female counterparts, even if they are a similar height and weight. This is considered to be due to the fact that males were evolved to do hard physical labour with their upper bodies.

Fortunately, it is possible for you to look feminine right down to your fingertips. You need to disguise the less ladylike aspects of your hands.

Keep your nails neatly groomed, that's the first rule. You can't change the size of your hands, but you can take better care of them. People always notice dirty, straggly nails. You don't have to grow your nails out, but do keep them clean and neatly shaped. Remove the hair from your knuckles as part of your hair removal routine. Sissies often forget about this simple and obvious detail. Women don't have hair on their hands, so take a razor or other preferred hair removal method and remove the hair.

Don't wear excessive jewellery near your hands, you might think that gold rings and bracelets make your hands look more feminine, but they call attention to an area that should be kept low key. Stick to the barest minimum of jewellery. Maids in fact often wear no jewellery at the order of their mistress.

If you do wear any jewellery, dainty rings and bracelets make your hands look even bigger in comparison. Wear chunky jewellery instead. There is no reason to hide your hands when you are dressed as a maid, except of course when you are wearing rubber gloves to do the dirty household jobs. It is important not to spotlight your hands with bad grooming and loud jewellery.

Heels are important for all women, so is it any wonder that most maids wear them, or that their mistresses may insist on them. Learning to walk in heels is a difficult task for new sissy maids! You will need to practise to be confident on your heels.

Here are some pointers to help you get started.

- The higher the heel, the greater the challenge, so start with a pair of heels no more than two inches. Once you've mastered that pair, try a higher heel.

- Before you take your first step, practice your balance by standing in heels. Experiment with different poses as you get used to the added height. Keep your shoulders back, your spine tall, and your chest forward. Good posture keeps you steady in the highest of heels. Now you're ready to walk! Take your first steps on a hard surface since carpet can throw off your balance.

- Beginning maids tend to turn their feet out as they walk, so remember to keep both feet perfectly parallel. Women walk with their legs close together, so imagine that you are placing each foot along the edge of a ruler - you shouldn't have more than two inches between your feet. Big steps can trip you up. Instead take small, delicate steps. The higher the heel, the shorter your stride should be.

- Bent knees throw off your balance and look inelegant. Practice walking with straight legs.

- Once you've mastered the basics, try turning in different direction. Take a few steps on different floor surfaces and practice your stride on stairs. Walking in heels is totally different from walking in tennis shoes, so don't expect instant success. Just keep practicing.

A small waist is essential if you are to look like a dainty maid. In fact, studies have shown that the greater the difference between a woman's waist and hips, the more attractive she is considered to be. Obviously, the less weight you have around your middle, the better.

For some maids, corsets can be uncomfortable to wear all day every day, although some mistresses may insist on this. Waist cinchers are designed to reduce your waistline while still allowing you more freedom of movement, they are worth considering if perhaps you need time to adjust to wearing a heavier, more restrictive corset. They are made with elastic and can take several inches off your waistline, although they are no real substitute for a boned corset. Look for waist cinchers with boning for the best results.

Most of us have poor posture due to being slumped over computers all day. There is no point in trying to look pretty and feminine if you have a large belly spilling over.

Good posture can instantly take ten pounds off your middle. Stand with your chest lifted, your shoulders back and your tummy in. This can make a huge difference to your overall shape. Belts, especially if they are wide, can act as waist cinchers if you wear them tight enough. However, there is nothing worse than seeing two big bulges of fat being squeezed out the sides of your belt. If this is a problem, the only solution may be the full, boned, Victorian style corset.

The size of your waist isn't as important as your overall proportions. The bigger your hips, the smaller your waist will appear. Padded knickers can give you extra curves, but you can also make your hips look bigger by wearing a full skirted maid's dress. Look for dresses with pleats or gathers around the hips to balance your proportions and make your waist look smaller in comparison.

Most sissy maids don't just want to look like maids, they want to look pretty. Unfortunately, the features of a beautiful female face don't come naturally to most males, particularly the traits of a delicate jaw and chin.

Try these four tips for disguising a manly jaw.

- When applying makeup, sweep a little bronzer or brownish-toned blush across your jaw line and chin.

This creates a shadow effect which makes strong features appear to recede.

- The purpose of a great hairstyle is to flatter your face by creating balance. Avoid straight hair or severe styles, as they will only make you look more masculine.

- Stay away from turtleneck or square necklines that accentuate a strong jaw. Instead, choose v-neck tops or rounded necklines to create a flattering frame for your face, although of course the type of uniform you wear may not give you options in this area.

- Nothing can transform your appearance faster than a wig. Wigs are the key to your success at looking pretty. But they are also a minefield of potential mistakes, so don't let a bad wig spoil all of your good work. Always invest in a good wig. Nothing looks more ridiculous than a cheap wig, so invest in the highest quality wig you can afford. A good wig feels soft and silky. In addition, your best bet is to choose a length and colour that flatter you. Choose a wig no more than two shades lighter or darker than your natural hair colour. This guarantees that the wig will work with your skin tone. It's easy to order a wig over the internet, but there is no way you can judge a colour or style from your computer screen. Find a wig shop and try on as many styles as you need to. Most wig shops have cross-dressing customers and will welcome your business.

Small feet are a coveted female trait for maids, but they don't come easy to most sissies. Men have proportionately larger feet than women, even if they are the same height. Try these tips to create the illusion of delicate feet.

Heels make feet look smaller because they bend the foot into a vertical position. Flats, on the other hand, highlight the broad expanse of your foot. Just don't go overboard if you are tall. People are a lot more likely to notice you towering over them than if your feet are on the large side.

Pointed toe shoes that were popular a few years ago are on their way out. Pointed toes add length to the foot, which is not what you need. Rounded toes are much more flattering. The more of your foot you expose, the larger it will appear, so strappy sandals should be avoided. Instead, you can show some skin by wearing peep toes or sling backs.

Light colours make an object appear larger, so avoid white, cream, or silver coloured shoes. Instead, look for styles in dark or subdued tones to downplay the size of your feet. Remember, keep your shoe styles simple and add flash to the areas you want to emphasise.

Some maids think the only way to enlarge the lips is with injections, but that's not true. You can plump your lips with some common kitchen ingredients, but first, here's why enhancing your lips is so important.

Full lips can distract from facial flaws like a big nose, square jaw or long chin. The bigger your lips are, the smaller your other features will look in comparison. Get some cinnamon oil or peppermint oil and add a drop or two to your favourite lip balm or lipstick. These ingredients increase blood flow to the lips, causing temporary swelling and a full, sexy pout. Dilute the oils since they can burn the lips if applied full strength. Also use plenty of moisturisers to combat dryness.

Remember the previous chapter where we discussed the corset and the hobble skirt. If you adopt that style of dress, it is certain that you will walk and generally conduct yourself like a lady. How can you do otherwise? You will be forced to take short steps, your hips will wiggle provocatively, and your body will be so enshrouded in garments that anything other than small, dainty movements will be impossible. You are already three quarters of the way there.

In days gone by girls practised deportment by walking with a book balanced on their heads. It is worth practising in this manner, and will help you look more feminine. How to models walk, you may ask? Here is a full description of how it is done.

- Be confident. A supermodel strut depends completely on confidence. You have to have a brave, commandeering walk to look like a supermodel. Push your shoulders back, this will add presence to your walk and elongate the neck. Push your pelvis forward, this will make your stomach look more concave and make your strut look more purposeful.

- Balance weight on the ball of the foot. This might be awkward because we usually balance weight on the heel. Keep the weight on the ball of your foot behind your toes, especially if you're wearing a tall, skinny heel.

- Keep those legs up. You want to take as long a step as possible. Lift your knee high and push it to the ground, almost spider-like.

- Point the toes in. Try to walk in a straight line, bringing one foot in front of the other as you move.

- Maintain a steady speed, and remember to keep your chin up. This ties in with the whole confidence thing and will keep your audience engaged.

You should consider your voice. Concentrate on pitch, resonance and annunciation. Pick a pitch just a little higher than your normal voice. Resonance is the timbre in your voice. Male voices have a lower resonance. Find the right one by speaking in the highest falsetto you can. Then find the lowest pitch in that range. Annunciation is the pace of your speech. Men tend to be more clipped. Women tend to curve and soften their speech.

Remember though, that 80% of communication is nonverbal e.g. -

- gestures
- movements
- expressions

Women tend to use their hands when they talk. They're more animated with their facial expressions. Just don't overdo it.

When standing, place your feet closer together, shoulders back.

When sitting, don't plop down like a man would. Gently does it.

Watch yourself in a mirror and you can also ask your mistress to watch and tell you when you are going wrong.

CHAPTER 7

The Training and Duties of the Sissy Maid

By training, we are talking about carrying out your duties as a sissy maid in a highly professional manner, so as to satisfy your mistress. That is your prime goal, to keep your mistress happy. The role of a sissy maid can often be difficult and uncomfortable, as well as physically tiring, but you must learn to ignore this and put your every effort into satisfying your mistress in every way. We intend to show you how a sissy maid can serve her mistress to the very highest standards. By this, we mean the way that you conduct yourself as a maid, always subservient to your mistress' requirements. Your mistress will tell you which duties you are to carry out.

The Traditional Duties of the Maid.

You should read this next piece carefully. It is based on traditional maid's duties as would be carried out in a Victorian household, with many modern touches, of course. However, just because time has moved on, this does not mean that the sissy maid should aspire to anything less than this level of work and conduct.

In brief, it is for the dutiful sissy maid to understand that she is to do cooking, waiting, and chamber-work, as well as the washing and ironing. She will perform all these duties herself. The maid may expect tuition with the laundry-work as she is unlikely to be experienced in this, and the lighter housework will need to be done quickly and efficiently as she goes along. It will be necessary to work quickly and neatly.

The maid must have a quick head and a willing heart, as she cannot accomplish everything in the work of the house without being very hard working and dedicated. The mistress of a maid must recognise this and be prepared to give the maid explicit instructions in the carrying out of her duties. Where the maid is slow or sloppy in her performance, she should be punished.

What her part is to be she must define as clearly as possible at the first, in order that the maid may know just what she has to do and be able to arrange her occupations to the best advantage. When the mistress does something outside of the duties she has assumed, she should have it thoroughly understood that her act is an exception, performed for some specific reason. It is very easy to let the exception glide into a rule, and what the maid received at first as a favour which would spare her extra toil she regards later as a right to which she is entitled.

At the beginning, the mistress will show the routine of the work of the day for the benefit of the new maid. After the maid has learned the ways of the house, she may find that she can carry out the work in her own way, which will render her work easier. She should be permitted to do so if the mistress finds that the tasks are discharged as well as under the earlier plan.

Certain regular duties are practically the same each day, no matter what the other work may be. Early rising should be insisted upon. Six o'clock is none too early for a maid to be up in a house where breakfast is at seven-thirty or eight o'clock. By half after six the maid should be dressed and down-stairs. The maid goes into the living rooms to open the windows and make certain everything is tidy. She may also brush out the front hall and sweep the garden path if necessary.

The maid then dusts the lounge and any other rooms in the house where she is required to do. The maid should straighten the furniture that is out of place, and brush up any scraps or dust that need to be removed. If the floors or parts of them are tiled she should go over them with a damp cloth.

Whatever else may be postponed until after breakfast, the dining room must not be over looked. It must be brushed up and thoroughly dusted. Few things are more unappetising than to sit down to the first meal of the day in a room which is untidy. If the maid is brisk about her work she can look after the lounge, hall and dining-room, and set the table before she has to go back to the kitchen. The dusting of the dining-room must never be omitted. The morning tasks may be lightened a little by setting the breakfast table overnight, and when this is done a thin cover should be thrown over the table after it is set to protect it from dust.

The preparation of breakfast is the maid's next duty. The extent of the work this involves varies in different households. In some homes there may be a full cooked breakfast, eggs or bacon, and coffee. In others, it may be a simpler affair of cereal and fruit juice. Whatever the breakfast it should be in ready at the hour appointed, if the mistress is on hand or not It need not be served until it is ordered, but it should be ready.

After the dishes have been removed and the rest of the breakfast served, the maid may be excused to go about her other work. The time of her own breakfast may be settled by the mistress and herself. The sensible course is for the maid to eat something and take a cup of tea or coffee in the intervals of her early work. If the maid prefers she can take her breakfast while the family is eating, but most maids and mistresses seem to find it more convenient to dispose of the bedroom work as early as possible.

When this is the case the maid should go to the bedroom as soon as the substantial part of the breakfast is on the table. The rooms may be brushed or gone over with a vacuum cleaner, not thoroughly, this comes at another time. The beds may now be made and the dusting done.

The maid may now take her own breakfast if she has not had it earlier, and clear the table. After every meal the dishes should be removed from the table as soon as possible. They should be carried into the kitchen, the cloth brushed, never shaken, and folded, and the dining-room put in order, the crumbs brushed from about the table, the chairs put in their places. The maid may now wash the dishes and then go back to her dusting and cleaning the bathroom.

To clean the bath-room properly, there should

always be strong cleaning materials at hand, a supply of cloths, a long-handled brush and a scrubbing brush. The hand basin, bath and toilet should be scoured out each morning. Use a long-handled brush. This enables the maid to clean the toilet. satisfactorily. Tap fittings and wood-work must be wiped off, the soap-dishes and toothbrush racks washed.

When the bathroom work is finished, the maid may return to the kitchen, wash and put away the dishes, and get the kitchen and pantries in order.

The mistress normally inspects the contents of the refrigerator and decides what shall be the meals for the day. Before, or after, such inspection the maid must wipe clean the shelves of the fridge and three times a week it must cleaned.

The general work of the house, of which more later, is undertaken now, and after it comes the preparation of lunch. At this meal little waiting is required. The table is set as for breakfast. If the work is properly managed there should be no heavy tasks for the maid to accomplish in the afternoon, except on washing and ironing days. They may perhaps attend to some light work like the polishing of silver, but, if her duties are arranged as they should be and she is brisk in their performance, she ought to be able to have a little time to herself in the afternoon. The preparation of dinner is seldom undertaken until after four o'clock in houses where dinner is served at seven.

The maid is expected to discharge the work of a regular waitress at dinner, so far as serving the dishes, passing plates, and the like are concerned and is not required to remain in the room, but to come when rung for. The work of clearing away and washing dishes is practically the same after lunch and dinner as after breakfast.

The usual costume of the maid in the early part of the day is a neat black dress and white apron, together with a suitable cap. While waiting at table they should wear white gloves and should additionally have a waterproof apron on when working in the kitchen, but there should always be a fresh white apron at hand to slip on when answering the mistress' bell. When dressed to wait at dinner the maid should put on a more formal black frock, white collar and apron and cap.

Washing windows is tiring, and the maid will feel it less if she does a few every day than giving a whole morning or afternoon to them. The polishing of furniture, silver and the cleaning of paint it is well to carry out all at one time and this may be done on Thursday, while the cleaning of the bedrooms and other parts of the house may be reserved for Friday. The woodwork about the doorknobs should be wiped off, the stairs brushed down or vacuumed, and the hall gone over with the vacuum cleaner daily, and the house, from top to bottom, thoroughly cleaned at least once a week.

How sissy maids should conduct themselves

Never begin to talk to your mistress unless it is to deliver a message, or ask a necessary question. Even then, do it as shortly as possible. Many maids who are fond of talking will make a common message an excuse for a long conversation. Never preface anything you have to say, but say it simply. By prefacing using some unnecessary beginning, as:-

"I was going to say, ma'am"
"I wanted to ask you, ma'am"
"I have been intending several times to tell you, ma'am"

Such beginnings are quite useless, and not only consume time, but sound familiar and awkward. Sometimes a kind mistress will ask questions and encourage a maid to speak about their own affairs. There can then be no harm in doing so. But if this should happen to you, remember two things. First, be sure you are careful to talk only as much as you see is agreeable to your mistress, and take the first hint to stop - such as your mistress' changing the subject, or sending you to do, or fetch something. Secondly, never think because your mistress has chosen to have a little friendly talk with you on one occasion - perhaps while she warmed her hands at your fire or while you helped her to undress - that she means to throw aside all reserve, and will like you to chat on in the same way another time, without encouragement.

The sissy maid should never speak when they go in to carry out any kind of chore in a room where the mistress may be sitting, either alone or with others.

There is, however, one little distinction to be made between your mistress and any other lady.

There may be many things you need to ask or to tell your mistress, and when there is something necessary to say, there can be no harm in speaking. But it should be done in a respectful way, not while you are kneeling to sweep or laying a cloth, but when you have done your work in the room, standing by the door. It is also better to speak on any domestic matter when your mistress may be in the kitchen, or even in her bedroom if you can manage it, rather than when she is in the drawing-room. In the kitchen or bedroom she is more likely to have her thoughts disengaged and at liberty to attend to domestic concerns.

Many occasions will arise when you will need to see your mistress without waiting for such an opportunity, and you will then be obliged to go in to her, provided you remember to stay as short a time as possible.

You should in such a case, go in and shut the door, standing by it, and it will be well to begin by saying,

"I beg your pardon, ma'am, but will you be so kind as to tell me — "

Do not fancy that any lady will think this strange or stare at you for saying it. It is only common civility. Maids always beg pardon or use some such words of apology, if they come in and speak unasked. If you feel shy at using these words of apology, you may still enter and speak in a gentle and respectful manner which shows you are sensible of intruding, a manner which implies an apology.

Always move gently. You must never run up and down stairs, unless you can trip down very lightly; but no one can run up lightly enough. However lightly you may go down, it should never be fast enough to make it difficult to stop. Your steps should never be heard, either on the stairs or elsewhere. Never rush in haste to the letter-box or anywhere. You should remember that as long as you are in service, you are always in the house of another. Always move as gently as the ladies do in the drawing- room. Avoid all kind of roughness and noisiness remembering that by being careless in this matter, you make yourself as troublesome as a noisy man.

Always stand still and keep your hands in front of you or at your sides, when you are speaking or being spoken to.

It is common to tell sissy maids to meet the eye of their mistress and look in her face while speaking to, or being spoken to by her. But it is better not to stare the whole time in a mistress' face but to look down occasionally, and look up on answering.

When answering the bell you should generally shut the door, and stand close to it while receiving your order. If no one notices you, stand till your mistress looks round. If she is alone or not talking, you may say, "Did you ring, ma'am?" but if she is talking, you must wait. It is not likely, however, that you will ever have to wait more than a minute or two, as someone in the room will be sure to see you if the mistress does not, and to call her attention to you.

Always stand up when the mistress comes into the room. This rule has, however, some exceptions. If you are at work and your mistress comes in merely to fetch something, without noticing you, it is not necessary.

If your mistress comes in, alone or not, and speaks to you always get up and stand till she has finished speaking. Should your mistress visit your bedroom rise each time she speaks to you or stand all time she is in the room.

If you are kneeling down to clean or sweep, and your mistress comes to speak to you, it will generally be enough to leave off working and rise half up, on your knees. A mistress who is with you often will not expect more.

Remember that as a sissy maid you are frequently required to serve in the very personal capacity of a lady's maid. For this you will need to be especially neat in appearance. This means taking extra care with your dress, your make-up and hair. Make sure your finger nails are always properly manicured.

Your daily duties as a lady's maid include helping your mistress dress and undress, and maintaining your mistress' wardrobe, including laundering the most delicate items. You may be expected to style your mistress' hair and possibly help her with her makeup.

Here is a summary of the kinds of duties the lady's maid should perform. Discuss with your mistress what she wants you to do and how you should go about learning to do those tasks that are new to you.

- To take care of the mistress in every way.
- Press all fine undergarments and blouses.
- Take care of the packing and unpacking.
- Light dress cleaning and all fine sewing.

- Carry in the breakfast tray.
- Run a bath for mistress.
- Lay out evening clothes, shoes, dressing gown and bedroom slippers.
- Go into each bedroom to tidy it, putting away clothes.
- Take away dresses to be pressed, underclothes to be washed and shoes to be cleaned.

As you will be the only maid in the household, you will have to take on the duties of housekeeping as well, duties that used to be performed by a number of maids with different roles. This means you will be very busy, of course.

Kitchen Maid

In the kitchen the sissy maid is expected to cook for the mistress and to wash the dishes after each meal. They are also expected to keep rest of the house clean and to take care of their own bedroom.

Parlour Maid

- Serving the mistress' meals.
- Setting and clearing the table.
- Washing the dishes after meals.
- Polishing and dusting.
- Arranging the flowers which must always be fresh.
- Sofa pillows plumped.
- Curtains drawn in the evening.

- The rooms must always look as though they've just been cleaned.
- Clean and polish the shoes of the mistress.
- Put away books and arrange magazines in a neat and presentable order.
- Care of the clothing, mending and small repairs.
- Clean bath and clean and tidy bathroom.
- Bring fresh towels when necessary, whenever the bathroom has been used. The bathroom should look as if it has just been prepared for the mistress' next visit.

Remember, as a sissy maid you are occupying a unique position in the household. In all probability your work will of necessity only be part time, so you will have to take care to make sure that you keep to your mistress' schedule at all times, with regard to your conduct, your dress and your carrying out of your duties.

Sissy maids should always be early risers and be ready with hot coffee, breakfast and the daily paper all served to their mistress on a tray in bed if so desired.

Sissy maids should pamper their mistress in every way

Sissy maids should always be ready, willing and able to massage mistress' tired feet, back and shoulders at their command or give a full body massage before or after work.

Sissy maids should assist their mistress in styling her hair for work or play and be capable of applying mistress' makeup, give her a manicure or pedicure, paint her nails and toes and give her a facial and remove unwanted body hair.

Sissy maids can help their mistress to prepare a household budget and shop for household goods and services if so ordered. This is at the whim of the mistress, not the maid.

Sissy maids need the occasional extra humiliation. The mistress should have her sissy maid put on their laciest uniform and invite her girlfriends over for a tea party and impress them with her sissy maid's skills.

The sissy maid can serve mistress grapes or strawberries and cream while she luxuriates in a scented bubble bath.

The sissy maid can perform business paperwork. While mistress relaxes, the sissy maid can type, work on the computer and prepare correspondences or do any other tedious business chores.

The sissy maid can serve as a personal secretary on the weekends. Fetching coffee or tea will be part of the sissy's job description.

The sissy maid can brush mistress' hair before bedtime as she unwinds.

The sissy maid can take good care of mistress' pets, brushing, feeding and walking.

CHAPTER 8

Punishment for the Errant Sissy Maid

Sissy maids often need to be punished and chastised, when they do not perform their duties to the required standard. Punishments can take a number of forms, from making the maid work extra hours and work harder and faster. Occasionally corporal punishment is required to bring the maid's performance up to the mistress' required standard. The sissy maid that comes on duty shoddily dressed, perhaps with a stained or dirty apron, make up or hair less than perfect, or any other transgression, will often need to be punished severely so that she does not make the same mistake in the future. A good thrashing will often give the desired result.

Here is an account of one maid's punishment.

The maid had spilled cigarette ash on the floor and had neglected to clean it up. Their defence was that they intended doing it, but just hadn't gotten around to it yet. It was obvious to the mistress that the sissy was destined to lose that argument.

She stood beside the seated maid and slowly raised the short, black satin skirt of her uniform to her waist and held it there. Below the lifted skirt she saw a pair of black nylon panties with clear skin showing around the leg bands, sleek, silken thighs made even whiter by the contrast of black suspenders attached to her corset which held clinging sheaths of nylon stockings around shapely legs. There would be more to be seen in just a little while. She took up the paddle and reached out to lower the maid's panties. She did it with dramatic slowness so that the twin mounds of the maid's buttocks were unveiled with almost maddening slowness.

"I think about twenty five on each cheek would be appropriate, don't you agree?" she said to the sissy maid.

"Yes, mistress," was the answer.

Mistress picked up the paddle and smiled as the sissy maid draped herself over the chair, ready to receive punishment. The mistress raised her right arm and brought the paddle down with a loud smack against the arched right cheek of the smooth bottom. She brought the paddle down sharply on the left cheek. This time her efforts were rewarded by a loud sob from the maid draped over the chair.

Mistress went on with the spanking. By the seventh smack the sobs had blended into a steady crying as the sissy heaved and tossed her mature buttocks.

This was an obvious mistake since mistress, quite adept at the art of spanking, soon adjusted her timing so that the paddle descended just at the right moment to meet the bucking hemispheres on their way up. In that way, she was able to make each spank sting more without expending a corresponding measure of energy.

Again and again was the sound of the smack.

"Damn it you hit too hard," shouted the sissy.

The last smack ignored the blazing red buttocks and struck the maid high on her sensitive thigh between the narrow suspenders. There was a higher pitched wail of protest and pain at that.

"That was for displaying anger and using improper language," the mistress took time to explain before going back to the stinging routine of adding redness to the twin hills that had changed from pale ivory to fiery red.

Suffice it to say that this particular maid learned

her lesson and was extra careful not to spill ash or anything else on the floor as she went about her duties. Another maid was generally sloppy about the way she carried out her duties, dusting left undone, cap not adjusted properly on her head, kitchen not cleaned properly after each meal. Here is how her mistress deals with her.

> *"You were sloppy again today, maid, you have not had a very good record in your housekeeping."*
> *"Oh, no, Ma'am, please do believe me, I did my best yesterday, and I thought I had left everything immaculate, just as you had told me to do."*

Knowing already that the she did not always make herself clear about how the duties should exactly be carried out, the mistress still felt it was her painful duty to carry out punishment, or perhaps the maids painful duty, but that did not mean she had to be severe. She therefore told the maid that she was sure she was sorry over having failed to carry out her duties properly, but a good punishment now would ensure that she would carry out her duties properly in the future. She then gently ordered her to go to the nearest end of the couch, bidding her bend well down over the heavy wooden arm and stretch her upper body along the couch.

She did so at once, not without more sniffling which she tried hard to suppress. From the shivering waves of tremors that rippled along their thighs and calves, and the tensions and contractions now taking place throughout her spaciously rounded, firm buttocks, it was not difficult to guess what apprehension the unfortunate girl was experiencing.

"How many am I to get, Ma'am?"

"Fifteen, maid. I think we had best get them over with, don't you?" the mistress said.

"Ouhh! Yes, I'll try to take them bravely, Ma'am."

"Get ready, then."

But the mistress had already decided to be less punishing and proceeded to apply the other spanks as lightly as she could, nevertheless the pale milky skin was streaked quite vividly. Then she told her maid to dress and that she would remember the punishment had been taken bravely.

CHAPTER 9

The Sexual Relationship between the Mistress and her Sissy Maid

As a sissy maid you will be expected, of course, to carry out certain duties of a sexual nature for your mistress. The roles of sissy maid and mistress are a fantasy world constructed to act out the innermost desires of both parties concerned. When the housework is done, the dishes cleared away and the ironing neatly pressed, both maid and mistress should look forward to a degree of erotic fun. It's healthy, happy and will keep you both attracted to each other and committed to the carrying out of your respected roles.

It will come as no surprise that people can become sexually bored with their partner and come to regard lovemaking as more duty than pleasure. Sometimes men will seek pleasure elsewhere and many women blame themselves when this happens. Some blame their partners. In actuality, blame is inappropriate. Men are wired to lose interest in a partner who's always available. They can't help it. Fortunately they're also wired to turn on to the techniques of female domination; they can't help that either. And the power of these techniques to excite is far greater than the tendency of monogamy to bore. The man who is part of a mistress and sissy maid relationship will have none of these problems. A sissy maid spends much of their time in a state of sexual arousal. They may find this frustrating at times, but always exciting and never boring.

Female domination saves a man from boredom, sexual boredom. A sissy maid is first and foremost, in love with their partner and the feeling doesn't go away. Many factors contribute to this, among them the same insecurity that keeps him sexually excited, her sharing of their vulnerability with respect to their female, sissy maid persona.

As with sexual excitement, only an uncommonly experienced and introspective man will understand that his enslavement is what makes him love his partner with such enduring intensity. The average man will be aware only of being in love. Both will be emotionally committed.

Intimacy

Men crave intimacy but fear it. Generally fear wins. A woman who sexually enslaves her lover can tip the balance so he can enjoy being known by her.

Early in a relationship, when a man is in love he wants to share all his thoughts, feelings, fantasies, beliefs, hopes, dreams and fears. He rehearses what he'd like to say, but typically can bring himself to voice only a small fraction of what's inside. He's learned to keep it all to himself, and the learning is of a sort that's difficult to overcome.

As the relationship matures, he feels obliged to control it. The necessity of confronting his partner as an adversary when they have differences (for that's how he sees it!) now makes self-disclosure impossible. The enemy might learn something she could use against him. This is war, and he has to win - has to expand and consolidate his control.

From her point of view, the most appealing aspects of his personality have disappeared behind an impenetrable wall. From his point of view he's involved in a relationship recognised as the ultimate in intimacy by his friends, colleagues, church and state and he's emotionally isolated.

Sexual slavery makes it easier for a man to talk openly with his partner about matters of emotional significance. It does this in several ways.

If she uses her sexual power to take control of

all aspects of the relationship, making whatever decisions there are to be made, he doesn't have to be ready for battle. There isn't going to be a battle, so there's no tactical disadvantage in having a history of intimacy.

If she considers his needs in making her decisions, and she would be foolish not to, he'll learn that it's in his best interest to let her know what those needs are. He'll learn to prioritise them honestly as well. Some things matter to him a great deal, others only a little. There are preferences he might insist upon in an ordinary relationship that aren't his at all, but represent instead what he thinks he owes his family or what he hopes will impress his mates. If she considers his stated needs in good faith, her decisions will suit him best if he's been honest with her. Intimate self-disclosure thus becomes a way of getting what he needs and wants.

Escape from Responsibility

Responsibility is strenuous. Some men, particularly those in high-pressure jobs that require them to make decisions that have profound effects on the lives of others, carry far more than is good for them. Such a man often feels relieved if his woman takes control of their relationship and assumes all responsibility for the part of his life that she shares. This type of man commonly becomes a sissy maid.

Permission to Reject Overwork

Some men, once married, spend too much of their lives working and too little at home. They do it partly because it's a socially acceptable way to avoid the terrors of intimacy, partly because they believe their wives value the financial rewards of their industry above their companionship. A few, sadly, are right. Most are wrong, but refuse to change their ways no matter how their wives beg. A woman who sexually enslaves her husband is in a position to require that he spend a reasonable amount of time at home. If she states a willingness to accept the resultant decrease in his income, he has no choice but to believe her. He's almost always happy with the results.

Motivation

By way of contrast, there are men who can't motivate themselves as they would like. They find it useful to have their partners oversee their endeavours, spurring them on with sexual rewards and punishments. Women may use the power of their femininity to push their men through a programme of weight loss, a course of study leading to a master's degree, training for a marathon or to the completion of a book of photographic essays! The men themselves will choose their respective goals and be happy for the motivational assistance their partners gave them, though they may grumble a bit along the way.

Knowing What is Expected

A man in a conventional relationship is often troubled by the feeling that his partner is unjustifiably annoyed with him, that she blames him for neglecting something important to her, for somehow failing to meet her needs. But she hasn't actually said that, and she certainly hasn't given him a list of things he's neglecting. Her rule seems to be, it's no good if I have to tell you, and he suspects that she changes the secret desideratum whenever he comes close to identifying it. He finds this frustrating.

The relationship between a dominatrix and her love slave doesn't work that way. She tells him clearly and truthfully what she needs, wants, and expects of him. He delivers it because he loves her. She thanks him. Simple and fair! Instead of feeling frustrated he feels appreciated.

Avoidance of Performance Anxiety

A man in a conventional relationship often falls into the worry that his partner will be horny when he's not, and that she'll react unpleasantly if he's unable to fuck her on demand. This worry kills what little desire he might have had, setting up a loop that can lead to chronic impotence.

A love slave doesn't have that problem, not unless his partner is foolish enough to demand sexual arousal from him. Instead he has the opposite problem, that he'll be embarrassed by his inability to keep his arousal under control. That mind-set precludes performance anxiety.

If she finds herself in desperate need of sexual satisfaction when he's absolutely incapable of arousal, she can always have him eat her or finger her, warning him beforehand what he's in for if he lets his cock get hard. Afterward she can congratulate him on his rare self control. This is not recommended this because it gets him used to the possibility of sexual contact without arousal, but it does get her needs met without inducing performance anxiety.

Games for the Mistress' Enjoyment

Women love a big strong man who can sweep them off their feet and carry them into the sunset. But you may be surprised to learn that one of the top female sex fantasies is to have that same big strong man serving them as a sissy maid, dressed and corseted in all of their frilly finery, begging for sexual release in the bedroom. One of the top mistress fantasies involves tying you down to a bed while she forces you to pleasure her with your tongue. The entire scenario revolves around you worshipping her body and begging for her attention.

There are so many sex games that mistresses and their sissy maids can play the lists are virtually endless.

Here is just a selection of subject areas that participants can explore:-

- adoration
- aggressive sex play
- alternative spirituality
- body worship
- bondage and discipline
- cruelty
- denial
- depersonalisation
- domestic service (the sissy maid)
- dominance and submission
- erotic boxing/wrestling
- erotic torture
- feminist spirituality
- fetishism
- flagellation
- foot worship
- forced feminisation
- forced chastity
- goddess worship

- gynosupremacy (female superiority) as a form of role playing
- humiliation and humbling
- masochism
- pain play
- personal services
- role playing
- sadism
- sensation play

That is just a small selection. Chastity is a frequent and popular game that mistress and maid can play. As previously mentioned this can satisfy mistress' typical fantasy, as well as provide extreme sexual excitement for the maid. Imagine being in a situation where every single one of your sexual impulses is going into overdrive, yet you cannot achieve the relief of ejaculation, perhaps because of a chastity device, perhaps because your mistress has forbidden it on pain of severe punishment.

Here is an excerpt from one particular story, illustrating the special arousal that can only come from chastity type restraint.

My mistress regarded me with a severe expression.

"You will have three weeks with this chastity device on you. You will not be able to have sex, masturbate or even get an erection. But the desire and inability for all those things will make you hornier than you can imagine."

I nodded yes and moaned through the gag.

I couldn't move and was so scared, I promised myself I'd do anything she wanted because she totally had me by the balls. Mistress then removed my gag and straddled my face. I licked her for a long time all over and she came several times, great physical reactions but not a word was said. She then dismounted my face and continued.

"You are my sissy maid for the rest of your life, or at least until I decide I don't want you anymore. Oral sex is the best and you will be giving me plenty of it. After those orgasms I'm feeling a little more charitable, so here's the deal.

If you're a good little sissy maid and keep me really happy at all times, at some point, I'll let you have sex with me. Don't get excited, you have a lot of learning to do and nothing is certain but it is normal after having your pussy sucked and licked to want to be filled by some hot hard cock. Of course, after seeing what you have to offer, you probably won't do, but even the lowest dog needs his occasional reward.

You will always refer to me as Mistress, even when we are with friends and family and you will do everything I ever say no matter how demeaning or disgusting you think the task.

If I'm ever disappointed with you, I reserve the right to refuse you relief, and if you ever upset me,

I will keep you locked in your chastity belt for long periods of punishment."

Mistress unlocked me and told me to get dressed. She went in to take a shower. It was pretty hard to concentrate on work while in the same house as my mistress. After she came out of the shower she called me upstairs. I entered the room sheepishly and said, "Yes Mistress?"

She was wearing just a towel. She told me to lie down on the floor on my back. I did and she stepped over my head and lowered herself onto my face. She said quietly "lick" and I did. After a few minutes she got really into things and totally shifted her weight from her legs to lean completely on my face, smothering me.

But, I continued licking her as she gyrated her pussy all around my mouth and face. After she screamed for a few seconds and squirted some of her juice down my throat, she got up and went into her dressing room - no "thank you" or "that was great" or "goodbye" - she just used me like a toy or a piece of furniture.

Then she came back and locked me back into my chastity belt.

"I was not satisfied with your performance, maid, so you will stay locked in that for the next six weeks. If by that time you have not improved, you will spend another six weeks without any sexual release. Do you understand me?"

"Yes mistress," I replied.

I no longer masturbate and I am permanently aroused and sexually frustrated. This does help me to stay focused on my mistress and serving her every need, and makes being her sissy maid bearable.

That is just a little example of how the sissy maid can serve their mistress and get satisfaction themselves in whatever way they prefer.

CHAPTER 10

Make up and Wigs

Foundation Creams. There are two types of foudation creams:-

- clear foundation cream that is applied in order to bind makeup preparations to the skin
- foundation cream that contains various colouring agents, which can be used to cover and disguise unwanted colouration on areas of the face

In this chapter, we shall deal with coloured foundation creams. Coloured foundation creams contain less pigment than cover creams. Therefore, when using foundation creams, the best cosmetic result will be achieved by proper selection of the right shade. This can be obtained by using only foundation creams and combining colour correctors with the foundation creams. If a foundation cream alone is to be used, one should keep in mind that it may appear darker in the container than when it is applied to the skin, because the pigment is in its concentrated form.

The undertones of the treated skin should be carefully analysed and identified in order to achieve the optimal colour matching.

If the foundation cream does not offer adequate coverage, a colour corrector can be used. Colour correctors are not foundations.

They are designed to be applied under a foundation in order to neutralize light-to-moderate skin discolouration. In such cases, only after the application of a colour corrector should one use a foundation cream which should more closely match the skin colour.

Colour correctors are most commonly used to counterbalance ruddiness or sallow under-tones of the skin. When using colour correctors, one should keep in mind some basic principles of proper colour matching:

- green corrector to conceal and neutralise pink or red skin discolouration
- lavender corrector to normalise a sallow shade
- gold corrector to tone down grey discolouration

Applying Foundation Cream

The foundation should be applied to the skin by lightly spreading it on, using a delicate swab or a disposable sponge (wet or dry), or with the fingertips. This spreads it out more evenly over the skin and helps it penetrate the skin pores, thereby improving its adherence to the skin so that it remains on the skin for longer. Once applied, the foundation should appear well blended.

Cover Creams

Cover creams are used to camouflage skin blemishes. They consist of various colouring agents in an oily base. The colouring agents give the product it's covering ability and, in various combinations, provide the required colour and appropriate degree of gloss. Substances used for this purpose include various minerals and metal compounds, such as titanium dioxide, iron-based com-pounds, zinc and magnesium compounds, and other pigments. As opposed to regular makeup products, cover creams are opaque, with superior covering capabilities. They are more stable on the skin, and remain on the face for longer than ordinary makeup products. This durability is particularly important when hiding scars. The reason is that the ability of a substance to remain on the skin for a long time depends on its ability to get into the skin pores. A scar does not have any pores, so ordinary makeup would normally not remain on scar tissue for a lengthy period.

To successfully match a cover cream to the maid's skin you must identify the underlying colours that make up the maid's skin tone. The procedure is performed as follows:

Identifying the Underlying Colours of the Skin.

- Hold a cover cream palette alongside the area of skin that is to be camouflaged. Make a quick scan of each cover cream shade to determine its match to the skin colour.

- If necessary, a second colour should be added and blended into the cover cream. No more than two cream shades from the cover cream palette should be selected to match the skin tone.

- Once the correct shade or shades have been chosen remove a small amount from the container and places it on the back the hand. The cream is rubbed onto the back of the hand in a circular motion until it is malleable and spreads easily.

- Three different colour combinations of no more than two blended colours are blended are to be mixed. Make a note of each formula.

- Try a small sample of each of the three separate cover cream combinations to the skin.

- Examine the maid's face from a distance and choose the best combination of cover cream. The cover cream should meet the edges of the surrounding skin without detection. If the cover cream colour combination is the right shade, it will blend so well (not too light or too dark) that it will barely be noticeable.

- If the cover cream colour combination is too dark, a little bit more of lighter colour of the two can be added until it matches the skin tone. A pinhead amount of white cover cream can also be used to lighten it

It is wise to test several different products to find the product with the optimal shade that is most suitable. To achieve optimal coverage, the makeup should be a little darker than the natural shade of the skin. (It should be remembered that the original shade of the makeup changes somewhat once it is applied to the skin, depending on the degree of moisture and the pH of the skin).

Applying Cover Cream

This involves the technique of dabbing on the cream with the third finger (or with a synthetic sponge) in a patting motion, rather than rubbing. The edges of the cover cream should blend with the surrounding skin to avoid areas of demarcation. The cover cream layer needs to be stabilised and waterproofed by the application of a colourless powder on its surface to prevent the cover cream from sliding on the skin. After the problem area has been covered, makeup should also be applied to the other side of the face in order to achieve a more natural and symmetrical look. Attempts should not be made to cover an area with the "perfect" coverage, which may give the face a strange and unnatural look. Every normal, healthy face has a certain degree of natural imperfection. Some examples of the use of cover cream are shown below.

The Correct Application Method

There are three distinct types of skin with regard to the level of moisture:-

o   dry
o   oily
o   normal

Each requires a different cover cream application method to ensure the best result.

Dry Skin

If the skin is dehydrated and dry in texture, the cover cream should be applied and left to remain on the skin for up to ten minutes before being set with powder. The powder should be colourless and quickly brushed off after application to prevent the area from looking scaly.

Oily Skin

The cover cream should be applied and powdered. The powder should be left sitting on top of the cover cream mixture for up to ten minutes to absorb the oils in the product before the powder is brushed off.

Normal Skin

The cover cream should be applied and powdered. The powder should be brushed off immediately to produce the most natural effect.

Wigs

No matter why you've decided to wear wigs, it's understood that you want them to look as beautiful and natural as possible. Natural hair wigs, unlike other mass-produced synthetic wigs, are constructed carefully and intricately, with the most advanced techniques. Thanks to the supreme attention to detail they are already, well on their way to looking like your original hair. But all faces and bodies are different, and what looks natural on a wig stand or model, may not look quite as nice on you when you bring it home. If you have purchased a human hair wig and want to make it look more like you, here are a few simple tips to achieve this.

1. Take your wig into the hairdresser's to get a trim. Sometimes all a human hair wig needs to look its best is a simple cut. A hairstylist can do this while you're wearing it to ensure that the new cut suits your face shape. A new cut for a wig can really go a long way and add a lot of versatility when it comes to styling. If there's a certain kind of style you like, but can't find a wig that mirrors it, you can also buy a longer wig and bring in a photo of the look you want.

2. Invest in some accessories. Hats, scarves and slides are all great ways you can feel more confident your human hair wig looks natural. Natural hair wigs will feel more and more like the real thing when you use some accessories. Changing your look is not only a great way to look more natural, it is a great way to have fun with your wig and personalise it.

3. Use brushes and combs specifically designed for wigs. It's more common than you think that someone would try and use a regular brush on their human hair wig. That is extremely detrimental to health and longevity of your wigs style. European hair wigs are weaved intricately and using a non-wire brush can give you a tangled mess. In addition to wire wig brushes and combs, you can invest in a hot comb. These are great if you want to put a little wave in a straight style or touch up your wig's curls.

4. Wash your wig with specially formulated shampoos and conditioners. European hair wigs require special attention when it comes to washing. You probably won't need to wash it as frequently as you would your regular hair, but no matter how often you plan on washing it, you should be using shampoo and conditioner for wigs only. Sometimes, conditioners for wigs often tend to be leave-in conditioners that spray. These are lightweight and can give your human hair wig that extra shine and bounce it needs after a wash. Cream conditioners can sometimes weigh the wig down and give it a greasy look if you use too much. So if you do use cream, use it sparingly.

Hair Pieces

Quality clip in hair extensions are several strands of hair, each attached individually. Usually three or four inch wide pieces go on the back of your head in several layers, and a few one or two inch wide pieces are put on the sides. As the name suggests, each strand is attached to your own hair with a clip. With a little bit of practice, clipping the extensions in becomes rather easy and takes only a few minutes. Taking them off is even easier.

You can usually find fourteen, sixteen and eighteen inch clip-in hair extensions. Anything longer puts too much tension on your own hair. Clip in hair extensions can be brought either made from synthetic fibre or harvested from human hair. The advantage of using human clip in hair extensions, as opposed to synthetic hairpieces, is that they can be coloured or used with heat such as straighteners or hairdryers. However the price is usually four times more expensive!

Clip in hair extensions are suitable for people whose natural hair is shoulder length or longer. If you have medium length hair, extensions can make it longer. If you have long but very fine hair, or your hair is not in its best condition, clip-in hair extensions are a great way to bring richness and fullness to your hair. They come in a range of colour and styles and usually made from synthetic fibres. So they are easily maintained.

Clip in hair extensions only look natural when they are mixed in with your natural hair, so if your hair is short people will notice that you are wearing extensions. If you have a short haircut, but are dying for long locks, buy a wig that is similar in colour to your natural hair. High quality designer's wigs look very natural and nobody will guess that you are wearing a wig, unless you tell them. If a wig is not for you, then you can go for salon-made clip in hair extensions that are braided or glued to your own hair. These stay in for several months, but cost significantly more than clip-ins.

Since clip in hair extensions are mixed in with your own hair, colour matching is very important. Human hair clip in extensions can be coloured to match your own hair colour exactly. However it is not recommended to do this at home, leave it to the professionals.

The cost varies greatly for human clip in hair extensions and clip in hairpieces, depending on the material. Synthetic hair extensions may cost you less than £25, but for real human hair extensions you may several hundred pounds. You can often find good discounts through online hair extensions and wigs shops.

Clip in hair extensions and clip in hairpieces can be real fun. They will help you to create a different image instantly, and can be a great self esteem booster.

CHAPTER 11

Skin Care

If our eyes are a window to the soul then our face is the home of our humanity. Your face is the first thing that people see. From an early age we learn the subtle cues that facial expressions share and look to the face as the true judge of sincerity. Over any other part of your body your face contains the richest source of information of who you are and how you feel.

The face is also the first place people look to confirm any suspicions they may have about your gender. Unfortunately many sissy maids fail this test because they lack a good skin care routine.

As a man you can easily get away with poor care

for your face. It's not by chance that the words rugged and handsome often find themselves in the same sentence. A weathered and time worn face denotes strength and wisdom in a man, but neglect in a woman!

Sissy Maid Skin Care Routine

To be considered beautiful by most of society a woman's face must resist the ravages of time and remain soft and supple. In our endeavour to emulate the feminine form we too must strive to provide loving care to our face – the ultimate cross dressing fashion statement. Use products tailored for your skin type. If in doubt about your skin type indulge yourself and have a facial at your local beauty salon where they will be able to tell you all about your skin type. To enhance and maintain your natural beauty there are five things you need to do as part of your cross dresser skin care routine.

Cleansing

Clean your face twice a day with a high quality cleanser. This will remove any excess dirt and oil and should make your skin feel fresh and a little tight. If your skin feels dry after washing your face check your cleanser, you may be removing too much oil. Do not use soap! Most soap is not good for your face.

Exfoliate

The skin goes through a natural cycle of dying and being replaced by new skin cells. Unless you do something about it dead skin cells will remain resulting in a dull and lacklustre appearance. The best way to stop this is to exfoliate once or twice a week after cleansing. This removes the dead layer of skin and will leave your face smoother and softer. Don't exfoliate more than twice a week.

Apply Toner

A toner helps freshen, soothe and condition your skin, helping it to better absorb moisture that you will apply next.

Moisturise

Men's skin is naturally coarser than a woman's. Sun exposure, smoking and drinking can quickly cause your skin to look old and tired. Moisturiser is essential to looking younger and keeping deep wrinkles at bay.

Apply Sunscreen

Sunscreen is essential if you're going out in the summer, even when it's overcast. Sissy maids struggle against their genetics as well as a lifetime of bad habits. Even if you've gone many years without taking care of your skin it is possible to reverse some of the damage. Following a regular routine of these five simple steps will allow your face to represent the pretty sissy inside you.

GLOSSARY

A

Abrasion - Dictionary term meaning a wearing, grinding, or rubbing away by friction. In BDSM play also stimulating the surface of the body with abrasive materials such as rough silk, leather, sandpaper, brushes, etc.

Age Play - Acting as if you were either younger or perhaps older than you really are.

Anal Beads - A set of strung beads used to insert into the anus to stimulate the anal nerves as foreplay or to cause orgasm.

Anal Play - This is generally play where the anus may be penetrated with either beads, ice, dildos, anal plugs, penis, or fist. Rimming the anus with a finger or toys stimulates the nerves which can create a more intense orgasm. Inserting and playing with one's prostate gland (males) will cause increased orgasm.

Anal Plug - A specially designed dildo used in the anus that is shaped in a way so that it will not fall out. Most commonly inserted and left in the anus for a given amount of time. Also used for "ass training" to stretch out the anus and get one accustomed to having something in their ass.

Anal Sex - Any sexual activity that involves the anus. Examples are; rimming (oral), Butt/Anal Plugs, Dildos, and penile penetration.

Animal Role Playing - Games in which one or more partners, usually the bottom, takes on the role of an animal. Most common is probably a dog, or puppy boy/girl though horses are also popular. The 'animal' may imitate animal behaviour, wear items such as collars, leads, bridles and so on, or carry out tasks associated with animal behaviour.

Arm/Leg Sleeves - Play which involves binding the arms/legs of the submissive in an attempt to restrict mobility.

Aromas - Play which involves the use of certain aroma therapy to induce relaxation, also referred to as "poppers". In some instances these can be volatile compounds whose vapours cause temporarily increased heart and breathing rates, muscle relaxation, and a "rushing" feeling in the head. These types of play are popular in the gay and rave scenes, and often used in an S/m context. There are some dangers associated with their use.

Asphyxiation - (See also Breath Control, Choking)

commonly referred to as "breath control". It refers to play involving the control of or restriction of air and / or oxygen to the brain. Any form of stopping breathing freely including choking, smothering and hoods with tubes, sacks, plastics, etc, is asphyxia. Sometimes it is used to cause a more intense orgasm. Other examples would be strangling which is compression of the neck or throat area to prevent oxygen to the brain; suffocation involves reducing the level of oxygen available to breathe; hanging where the body is suspended by the neck (remember, all these games are extremely dangerous, either alone or with a partner, and may cause DEATH).

Auctioned for Charity - Involves play where the partner (usually the submissive) is auctioned off to others for charitable purposes and or services to another. This is illegal in many areas.

B

Ball Stretching - Play which involves a type of penile constraint attached to weights in order to provide a variety of sensations including discomfort and pain, while stretching the testicles and scrotum.

Bathroom Use Control - Scenes where the dominant restricts or takes control over the submissive's bodily functions through the use of techniques such as catheterisation, enemas, diapers, rubber pants and possibly golden showers. Examples in play: House training a puppy, age play, and golden shower play.

Bestiality - Play which incorporates the use of animals for sexual pleasure. Not to be confused with animal role playing. This form of play can be very dangerous.

Beating - Striking the body with various objects or the hand. Typically administered as punishment in connection with childhood punishments. For example, the dominant may administer a beating to an unruly submissive.

Being Serviced (sexually) - Play which involves just that. The dominant instructs the submissive to do exactly how he/she wants the submissive to perform sexually.

Biting - Scenes involving the biting of the skin to induce pain. Safety Note: Although certain types of nibbling/biting are quite safe, extreme biting causing breaking/bleeding of the skin is not recommended and can be dangerous if not carefully done.

Blindfolds - Play which involves temporarily blocking the submissive's sense of sight. This type of play is essential when everyday objects are used to give unexpected sensations. Blindfolds come in many forms from the more expensive leather (full-head type) to the more inexpensive handkerchiefs, scarves, bandages. Safety Note: Do not make the blindfold too tight as to put pressure on the eyeballs. Although some people take blindfolding in stride, it can have unpredictable psychological effects and be extremely frightening for some people.

Breast / Chest Bondage - The restriction/bondage of the woman's breast/chest area for erotic reasons, using various types of fastenings (rope, scarves, etc.).

Breath Control - Refers to play involving control of or restriction of air and/or oxygen to the brain. Other examples would be strangling, which is compression of the neck/throat area to prevent the flow of oxygen to the brain. Suffocation involves reducing the level of oxygen available to breathe; hanging where the body is suspended by the neck (remember, all these games are dangerous to play, either alone or with a partner).

Branding - Making a permanent or semi-permanent scar on the skin by burning it with a hot metal object, as practiced on livestock. Seen by some as body art, this technique can be carried out safely; however, it is still likely to be intensely painful. Can also use temporary tattoos or markers. Used by dominants to mark their property. Not for the novice.

Boot Worship - The practice of play involving a fetish for boots/shoes. Commonly used for domination and humiliation practices (licking or cleaning of the dominant's boots, shoes or bare feet).

Bondage - The restriction of a person's bodily movements for erotic reasons using fastenings of various types or textures. Also used in S/m practices. Examples; rope, cuffs, chains, and other restraining apparatus.

Breast Whipping - Whipping of the woman's/submissive's chest area using a variety of items which include: floggers, whips, cat tails, paddles, for erotic purposes.

Brown Showers (Scat) - The practice of play involving a fetish for including human (or animal) faeces. Although this type of play can be safe if done correctly, it is not recommended for those faint of heart!

Bruising - A condition which may occur as a result of pinching or striking. Care should be taken to avoid bruising.

C

Cages - Most common is the use of a large animal cage. Construction of a cage can be of wood, steel, fencing material. Used to confine the submissive, for play or punishment.

Caning - Mostly made of bamboo, this whip is by far the most painful. Care should be used, as the welts from caning are slow to rise, and blood can be accidentally drawn if not in constant monitoring. Caning should be limited to the fleshy part of the buttocks, and nowhere else on the body. This can be very dangerous, and is not for the novice.

Castration Fantasy - There has been much confusion as to the actual meaning of this term. This refers to removal of the testicles; however, some people use it for the removal of any/all sexual organs of either sex. The removal of the testicles is sometimes referred to as Emasculation and a man who has had his testicles removed is referred to as a eunuch. This procedure causes permanent and significant changes to the body. Castration fantasies are actually quite common among the heavy S/m players and are played out in scenes involving cock and ball torture (CBT), permanent and play piercing, and even genital shaving. However, few people actually choose to make this fantasy a reality. It should be noted here that this is a serious surgical procedure and not something someone can teach themselves to do safely. This form of play is very dangerous.

Catheterisation - A flexible tube used in medical procedures generally inserted into the area controlled by the bladder. This procedure is most often used for "control" scenes.

Cattle Prod - An electrical prodding device used to herd animals, more frequently for cattle. Sometimes used in S/m play for "branding" or serious hardcore pain play, and is considered dangerous play.

Cells or Closets - Play which involves locking the submissive in a cell-type device and/or closet. Usually as a form of punishment. Not recommended for claustrophobics.

Chains - A strong metal type of bondage material used in bondage scenes. Chains are less flexible and potentially more dangerous than other types of bondage material.

Note: Always make sure you observe metal bondage rules and choose a chain and equipment that will withstand heavier strain.

Chamber-Pot Use - Scenes involving the use of the toilet for humiliation and/or control. Generally used for medical scenes.

Chastity Belt - In S/m circles meaning the banning or physically preventing one (male or female) from achieving orgasm or any form of genital stimulation. A means of domination over one's submissive. A device (lockable) panty-type which when worn prevents any type of genital stimulation.

Chauffeuring - Requiring one's submissive to "chauffeur" them around physically in vehicles or other types of transportation.

Choking - Compression of the carotid arteries in order to restrict air or blood flow to the brain.   This form of play is dangerous.

Chores (Domestic Service) - Scenes where the dominant requires the submissive to perform chores and/or domestic service in either sexually pleasing clothing (maid outfits) or naked.

Clothespins - Small pinning devices used for hanging clothes. Generally used in BDSM play as quite effective nipple clamps, testicle clamps, etc.   Great for the bargain BDSM player!   Ensure the wood doesn't become stuck to the skin while removing, as it will remove skin from body.

Cock & Ball Torture - any form of restraint or orgasm control to a male's genitals. Can be used for play or punishment.   Not for the novice, as this can be dangerous.

Cock Ring - Rubber, metal, or leather type ring used to strap around the base of the cock and balls when soft.   Increases blood flow to the genital area during self stimulation and sex. When released, causes minor pain during recurring blood flow.

Cock Worship - Play which involves the fantasy of worshiping the cock.   Performed mostly by the submissive to the Dominant.   Scenes might include licking and/or fellatio. Even some female Dominants may use strap-ons that are worshipped by the submissive male or female.

Collar - A collar worn around the neck to indicate one's submissiveness. These can be made of leather, steel, rubber, rope.   Used in scenes for humiliation and/or examples such as dog/puppy or even boy/girl play.

Competitions - Scenes involving competitive-type sports or play with other submissives.

Corsets - A lingerie / binding type device worn to restrict the chest area and make the waist smaller. Worn by early 19th Century women as a form of formal dress to make one's self more appealing to the opposite sex.

Crotch Torture - Any form of torture to the male or female genital area.

Cuffs - A leather or metal bondage device used to restrict movement.   Usually locks around the limbs in order to place the submissive in a precarious position.

Cutting - Cutting the surface of the skin with sharp objects, generally a knife, for the thrill, sensation, or pain.   To also create decorative scars.   The same basic precautions apply as with other types of blood play.   Remember to stay away from vital organ areas and genital cutting.   See also Abrasion, Branding, or Castration Fantasy.

D

Diapers - Waterproof panties or cloth worn in BDSM play for the object of child-playing scenes. Also used in control scenes for controlling bodily functions.

Dilation - The term used when a woman's cervix is dilated (opened) to aid in childbirth. In BDSM play dilation occurs when a speculum (pelvic exam device) is used to open the cervix. Safety Note: Care should be exercised and previous study should be done, before attempting this play. This form of play is dangerous

Dildo - From the French term meaning "I please myself". A phallic-shaped device designed for insertion into the body. Early versions were made of stuffed animal gut, leather, or ceramics; however, today they are most commonly crafted of moulded latex. They may be hand-held, strapped on with harnesses to allow women to wear, or permanently placed on other devices to ensure stability during use. Hygiene demands that dildos not be shared with others, or condoms be placed on dildos to prevent the spread of STD's.

Dominant - The one in charge, or the top who oversees and controls. A dominant should be well versed in many areas of sexual play for safety. The Responsible One.

Double Penetration - Play involving the penetration of two or more bodily orifices with various types of devices and/or genitalia, (i.e., penetration of the mouth/rectum/vagina, etc.)

E

Electricity - Using electricity in BDSM play seems a scary notion to most people, but it can easily be made safe provided two simple rules are followed: a) only use devices powered by low-voltage batteries, and certainly no main-powered appliances; and b) avoid placing any contacts above the waist (including hands or arms), as even small currents to the heart or brain can disrupt those organs' delicate electrical activity with serious consequences. Popular devices include "TENS" units designed for the relief of muscle and back pain; and "Violet Wands" which use a radio frequency discharge, and can be used above the waist provided the face is avoided. Any form of this play can be dangerous.

Enemas - A thorough anal cleaning involving a water bottle and tube. Most frequently used medically although might also be used for control scenes as well.

Enforced Chastity - In BDSM/S/m circles, meaning the banning or physically preventing one from achieving orgasm or any form of genital stimulation. A means of domination over one's submissive. A device (lockable) panty-type which when worn prevents any type of genital stimulation. See also "Chastity belt"

Erotic Dance - Scenes involving erotic dancing/ stripping as a form of erotic pleasure; i.e., to music.

Examinations - Scenes involving some type of physical examination (i.e. medically) where the use of various types of equipment are used. Safety note: Genital examinations should be done carefully, as serious consequences could result if not performed carefully. This form of play can be dangerous.

Exercise - Play which involves forcing one's submissive to exert physical exercise as a form of control/humiliation (may include lifting, running, weight-lifting, etc.).

Exhibitionism - Common dictionary term meaning

a perversion marked by a tendency to indecent exposure; an act of such exposure; the act of practicing or behaving in such a manner as to attract attention to oneself.

Eye Contact Restrictions - Restricting one's submissive from any eye contact with the Dominant (i.e., forcing submissive to look away / look down). Similar to military boot camps. Control is enforced by the dominant by refusing eye contact.

F

Face Slapping - Involves play where a moderate amount of slapping of the face is used for humiliation/control. This play can be dangerous if an eye is struck, etc.

Fantasy Abandonment - Play which involves the fantasy of abandonment. Possibly leaving the submissive in a deserted area or public area for a short period of time to exert control and punishment.

Fantasy Rape - Scenes where the dominant fulfils a submissive's fantasy of rape.

Note: This type of play can become quite emotional for the submissive, so use extreme care when performing this type of play. After care is extremely important

Fantasy Rape (Gang) - Involves the same type of play (Fantasy Rape) with the exception of scene being performed by a group.

Fear - Incorporating fear into scenes by using the submissive's own fears as an outline for play. Note:

This type of play can become quite emotional for the submissive, so take extreme care when performing this type of play, and aftercare is important again

Fellatio - Performing oral sex on a man's penis.

Fisting (Anal/Vaginal) - Play which involves placing or attempting to place the entire hand (or even both hands) in the rectum/vagina. The hand is only formed into a fist, and once fully inserted, requires an extreme gentleness, care and patience. Involves moving of the fist in and out of the orifice and can be a dangerous technique if not performed correctly. Proper study should be done before attempting such, and after care is extremely important. This form of play is dangerous.

Flame Play - Play which involves the use of fire. It should be noted here that using any type of fire/flame is quite dangerous and could result in permanent scarring/burning of the body. Use extreme care when using fire in scenes, as this is extremely dangerous and not to be done by a novice.

Flogger - A whip device usually with many "tails". Used on buttocks or back, generally to make nerve sensations greater. Floggers can be used on the genital areas. Can be used for play or punishment. This form of play is not for the novice, and can be dangerous.

Flogging horse - A device used to secure one on this bench-like, padded, sawhorse. Usually made waist height, with the use of tethers attached to wall or floor to secure the submissive. A well designed horse will allow open spread usage of the submissive when mounted properly upon.

Food Play - Where the dominant controls amount and type of food allowed to be consumed by the submissive. This includes liquid intake as well.

Foot Worship - The practice of play involving a fetish for feet. Commonly used for domination and humiliation practices (i.e., licking / cleaning of the dominant's feet).

Forced Bed Wetting - Forcing the submissive to purposely urinate in the bed. Most commonly used as a form of control / humiliation and in age play scenes.

Forced Dressing - Forcing the submissive to dress however the dominant sees fit, whether publicly or privately. Used generally for humiliation.

Force-Feeding - A technique by which the dominant controls the submissive's eating habits. Used to "fatten up" submissives or in age play games.

Forced Homosexuality - Scenes where the submissive is forced into having sexual relations with someone of the same sex.

Forced Heterosexuality - Play involving the submissive performing forced sex with someone of the opposite sex.

Forced masturbation - Scenes where the submissive is forced to perform masturbation in front of/for the Dominant or others as a form of erotic/sensual play or humiliation.

Forced Nudity - A scene which involves forcing one's submissive to remain nude either privately or publicly. Generally as a form of control/

humiliation. Note: In some areas, this is illegal in public.

Forced Servitude - A form of play involving the submissive acting as a servant/maid to the Dominant. May be played out in public or in private as a form of humiliation.

Forced Smoking - Forcing the submissive to smoke (usually cigarettes); however, other various types of smoking are used in heavy S/m play.

Full-Head Hoods - A flexible covering for the head and sometimes neck. These come in a variety of shapes, sizes, and textures. Worn to prevent the sense of sight for erotic purposes.

G

Gags - To restrict the use of the mouth by inserting a gag, in various textures (i.e., cloth, leather, ball gag, etc.). When using gags, it is important to remember that these only be worn for short periods of time. This form of play can be dangerous.

Gas Mask - A mask worn on the face connected to a chemical air filter and used to protect the face and lungs from toxic gases. Used mostly in heavy S/m sceneing.

Gates of Hell - A type of cock ring worn around the base of the testicles and penis to restrict blood flow to the penis during erotic sceneing. Specially designed, this type of cock ring is usually made of metal and has several rings attached together, ranging from the largest at the base and going smaller toward the tip.

Genital Sex - To cause an orgasm through the genital area, done strictly to the genital area with any body part or through the use of toys.

Given Away - Where a dominant releases a sub to another dominant, without exchange of favours.

Golden Shower - Play which involves urinating on one's submissive or vice versa.

Gun Play - Scenes involving the use of firearms. It should be noted here: Gun play is a dangerous form of play and should not be entered into lightly. Serious consequences could occur from such play and it is not recommended. It is also considered illegal.

H

Hairbrush Spanking - Play which involves the use of a hairbrush to inflict pain on the buttocks. Commonly used in "naughty boy/girl" scenes for punishment.

Hair Pulling - Pulling of one's hair for the purpose of pain/humiliation. Used often in heavy sceneing.

Hand Jobs - Using the hands to perform sexual gratification on a man's penis. Stroking of the penis to facilitate orgasm.

Harem - To have more than one submissive in a scene or in daily life (i.e., the Dominant has a "harem" of women/men). A common occurrence in the Mormon religion, and in polyamorous relationships.

Harness - Bondage apparatus consisting of a

network of straps designed to form a web over a large area of the body or head. Well-known leather body harness for wearing around the upper torso. Harnesses can be constructed from a variety of materials. Some harnesses built properly are used in suspension.

Head - To perform oral sex on the man's penis for erotic pleasure to facilitate orgasm.

High Heels - Along with boots, these are the most fetished items around. They combine the discomfort and pain of wearing them with the damage they can inflict when used as weapons. Some scenes may involve wearing, licking, cleaning, etc. See also "Boot worship"

Homage - Term meaning to pay respects to; homage; honour. A ceremony involving the submissive "honouring" the Dominant in some way - public or private. Could also mean paying "homage" to the penis/vagina, feet, breasts, etc., by worship.

Hot Oils - The use of warmed oils for massaging or various other uses for erotic type play. Be careful of oil temperature before applying to another's skin, test on your own forearm first. This form of play can be dangerous.

Hot Wax - The process of using hot wax in sceneing. The wax most commonly used are candles and can be used on various parts of the body for erotic stimulation. Note: Some types of wax, beeswax for instance, have a tendency to become extremely hot during burning and should always be used carefully to prevent permanent burning/scarring of the skin. Note: not for the novice, as this form of play is extremely dangerous.

Housework - Play involving the dominant instructing the submissive to perform domestic duties as a form of punishment/control. Can sometimes also be used as erotic play (i.e., cleaning in the nude).

Humiliation - To humiliate the submissive by requiring them to perform things they normally would not do, most commonly in public (i.e., wearing revealing clothing; having sex in public; playing out puppy, boy/girl scenes, etc.).

Hypnotism - To place someone in a trance-type state, and offer suggestions into certain types of behaviour. Safety note: This form of play is not for the novice.

I

Ice Play - ice used on nipples or genital areas for desensitisation of senses or nerves.

Immobilisation - Any form of bondage technically immobilises someone; however, this term is usually used for extreme forms of bondage where the submissive literally cannot move a muscle. Not recommended for long periods of time, and is dangerous.

Infantilism - Sceneing where the submissive assumes the role of a child/infant and is treated as such (i.e., diaper wearing, spankings, standing in corner, etc.).

Initiation Rites - A term meaning the rites, ceremonies, and/or ordeals by which an individual is made a member of a house or society. Example: College initiations.

Injections - Term meaning to inject the body with a substance (i.e., saline solution, insulin, flu shots, drugs, etc.). Usually performed with a hypodermic needle.

Note: This is a very risky type of play and is NOT recommended. The sharing of needles should never be done! Injections should be left to those that have been properly trained or to health care professionals. This form of play is dangerous and is illegal in most countries.

Intricate (Japanese) Rope Bondage - A very complex form of bondage that is also quite beautiful to not only see but witness being performed. The submissive is also bonded in such a way as to allow easy access/removal of the device at any time.

Interrogations - Term meaning question, systematically and formally. Commonly performed in "police interrogations"; police-type sceneing. Commonly used for humiliation.

K

Kidnapping - Term meaning to seize, detain, or carry away by unlawful force. Some players in the BDSM scene have fantasies regarding kidnapping and may ask for a scene involving some sort of "play kidnapping". This form of play requires after care and is classified as illegal in many areas.

Kneeling - To be used as a form of respect toward the dominant. Making the submissive kneel when the dominant enters the room, during sceneing, in public, etc. A punishment form of kneeling is where the submissive is kneeling in a different position then for offering herself.

L

Leather - Material made from the cured skin of animals. Wearing leather is a popular sexual fetish. Leather, especially the wearing of black leather gives the wearer a certain sense of power and is commonly worn in the BDSM scene by the Dominant. Used for making floggers, whips, etc

Licking - Play involving the licking of various body parts.

Lingerie - Women's intimate apparel. Lace bodices, stockings, bras, panties, etc.

M

Manacles/Irons - Metal rings joined by a chain to restrain the wrist or ankles.

Massage - Using the hands (generally) to massage areas of the body. Possibly giving a massage to warm up or foreplay before play.

Medical Scenes - Done in a room equipped and fitted as a physician's or surgeon's office. This is a form of role play, where cavity examinations, piercing, the use of needles, scalpels, equipment sounds are generally found. Not for the novice. Some forms of this play is illegal, and can be dangerous.

Mentor - One who assists another in study. Usually a well-versed dominant helping a submissive understand the lifestyle and their role in it. A mentor guides another to achieve knowledge, not a teacher.

Modelling - Usually used for pictures, where one is placed in positions for best appearance

Mouth Bits - A type of mouthpiece, generally used on horses and ponies that is inserted into the mouth and is used to bite down on. Used typically during pony girl/boy play scenes.

Mummification - A specialised kind of bondage in which the whole body, including the head if a breathing tube is used, is wrapped tightly to prevent any type of mobilisation. Common types of materials are saran wrap, gaffer tape, or cloth or latex bandages. Holes are then sometimes made to allow access to the genital area. This form of play is dangerous, and should always have extra help around in case of an emergency.

N

Nipple Clamps - Clamp-type devices placed on the nipples during play to stimulate and stop blood flow to the nipple. General household items to be used are clothes pegs. Care should be exercised to be sure the material used in clamp does not stick to the skin, as tearing can occur.

Nipple Rings - A ring that is worn through the nipple. Piercing of the nipple and inserting a ring, similar to nose piercing. This type of piercing stimulates the nipple. Should be done by a professional.

O

Orgasm - Intense excitement resulting in an explosive discharge of neuromuscular tensions at the height of sexual arousal that is usually accompanied by the ejaculation of semen by the male and by vaginal contractions in the woman.

Orgasm Control - When one is forced to release or hold their body's desires to orgasm. Can be used in play or punishment.

Outdoor Scenes - Scenes involving the great outdoors! Some activities are illegal.

P

Pain - In broad terms, pain is the body's warning that something is wrong. However, our pain responses are very complex and it is very easy to produce the effect of pain without doing any real harm to the body. The pain threshold at which a stimulus crosses the boundary between intense sensation and pain is a grey area in terms of our perception. BDSM is associated in most people's minds with potentially painful activities, sometimes referred to as "pain games". It is true, however, that some people actually enjoy or at least get some satisfaction out of the intense physical sensation. Some of the satisfaction may be attributed to the release of body chemicals also known as endorphins. Most players' interests are a mixture of physical aspects and the psychological dynamics of domination and submission, and some play with hardly any physical pain at all. Those for whom the interest in pain is predominant are sometimes referred to sadists and masochists rather than dominants and submissives. After care is needed, and monitoring the one receiving pain is mandatory. Not for the novice.

Parachute - Round leather device which is fitted between the scrotum and the base of the

penis with chains for weights to be added. This is a form of play, or punishment.

Phone Sex - Play which involves having simulated sex over the telephone. Some phone companies deem this illegal.

Piercing - Piercing of the body with a thin sharp object such as a needle. There are two types of play, permanent and temporary. Permanent piercing is done with a thicker needle which enables jewellery to be easily inserted. Temporary piercing is done with a smaller, thinner needle which can be removed without permanent scarring after the session is completed. (nipple, ear and genital piercing). Mostly done to enhance the sensual areas of the skin. Piercing should be done be a professional.

Pony - A device used directly on genitals for punishment. The person's body weight plus additional weight is placed directly on the pony which distributes pain to a particular area. This is extremely dangerous as permanent damage may result. Not for the novice.

Pony Gear - This type of gear includes hoods, bits for mouth, bridles, straps, harnesses, saddles and anal plug tails. Some use hoof shoes as well. These are used to train a submissive to be used for work, as a pony. This can be very dangerous as joints, limbs or back maybe damaged. Not for the novice.

Pony Slave - Scenes involving the submissive being dressed or made up to portray a pony. Scenes might include mouth bits, harnesses, saddles, riding crops, etc.

Note: Riding your pony can cause serious damage to their backs, hips and joints.

Prison Sceneing - Acting out a scene involving some type of prison scene. The use of a cell is for punishment and humiliation.

Prostitution - The selling of one's body for sexual purposes (i.e. selling sex or sexual favours). This form of play is illegal in many areas.

Public Exposure - Play which involves exposing oneself in public (i.e. flashing). Used for control/humiliation purposes.

Punishment - Scenes where the dominant punishes the submissive for bad or unruly behaviour. Often performed in little boy/girl scenes which may involve spankings, time-outs, etc.

Pussy Whipping - Whipping the genital (vagina) area with different types of equipment (i.e. floggers, crops, slappers, etc.) for erotic pleasure.

Pussy Worship - The practice of play involving the worship of the female genitalia. Scenes may involve the cleaning, licking, shaving, etc. In general, worship is a form of erotic play.

R

Rack - A table-like device which is fitted with pulling or stretching capabilities. Some racks incorporate pulleys, winches or wheels for pulling one in opposing directions. Paddles or whips are generally used on the person on a rack.

Religious Scene - A form of play where the submissive is usually dressed in nun's or clerical attire.

Riding Crop - A short whip-type instrument made of leather with a loop at the end which is intended for use on horses. It may be used in scenes involving pony/ boy/girl type play. Riding crops are used to administer punishment as well.

Rimming - Mouth contact with the rectal area, which includes insertion of the tongue.

Note: Hygiene precautions should be observed with this type of play. This play can spread disease.

Rope Bondage - There are many styles of rope work from simple to very intricate. Study of knots is important to anyone wishing to attempt this play. This form of play can be very dangerous if blood flow is disrupted. Not for the novice.

Rubber/Latex Clothing - Besides leather, this type of clothing is the next best thing. One example may be a rubber hood. Some bondage items are made out of latex sheeting, and as with leather, black seems to be the most popular colour.

S

Saint Andrew's Cross - This is a cross made in an X formation. It is generally angled and self-supporting. Some are suspended from ceilings or mounted directly to a wall. The cross has leather restraints for arms, legs and body. Some have hooks along the edges for a person to be laced to the cross. Used for sexual play, or punishment can be administered while attached to the cross.

Saran Wrap - Plastic wrapping used most commonly to wrap leftover food. In BDSM play used most likely in bondage scenes. This form of play can be dangerous.

Scratching - Scratching the body with the fingernails or another instrument for mild pain. Note: Safety precautions should be observed as deep scratching may lead to bleeding of the skin. Care should be exercised in preventing infection.

Sensory Deprivation - Play which involves depriving the submissive of certain sensory perceptions. May include blindfolds, bondage, gags, etc.

Shaving - Using a razor or straight blade to shave hair from the body.

Note: Shaving of the genital area should be done with extreme care.

Shibar - The art of Intricate Japanese Rope Bondage. Bondage patterns are intricate and artistically pleasing.

Skinny Dipping - Refers to swimming in the nude/ naked.

Slave - A totally subordinate person who needs total direction in all aspects of their life. To be owned, to serve, without question, and who questions nothing they are told.

Sleep Sack - Refers to a bag in which the body is wrapped in a sleeping bag type contraption with ropes or straps. An intense form of bondage. This form of play can be dangerous.

Slings - Slings are made in many designs and shapes, but their use is to open access to the genitalia for play or punishment. This form of suspension causes fatigue rather quickly, so after-care should be taken as well as care during such use. Not for the novice.

Spandex - A form-fitting, stretchy type material that clings to the body (most women's pantyhose are made of spandex). When worn can be quite comfortable and look extremely sexy when worn on "tight bodies".

Spanking - Involves striking someone with the palm of the hand or other object (paddle, hairbrush, pig slapper, riding crop, etc.) on the buttocks as a form of punishment/humiliation. Mild spanking can be very erotic and when done correctly can push the submissive into "subspace" releasing endorphins which in turn creates a sense of euphoria.

Speculum - A medical instrument intended for the use of medical examination of the vagina or rectum, made of steel or plastic in the shape of a duckbill. The speculum is lubricated and inserted. After insertion, the bill is spread apart to open the cervix in the vagina. In BDSM play commonly used in medical sceneing. This form of play can be dangerous. Not for the novice.

Spreader Bar - A bar type device used to spread apart arms/legs of the submissive. Bars can be made of common, inexpensive materials such as dowel rods, pvc pipe, broomsticks, etc.

Stocks - A type of bondage furniture based on the medieval form of stocks used for punishment. Stocks usually consist of two hinged pieces of wood with semi-circular holes which when locked together form a ring large enough for the head/neck and wrists to be placed inside.

Straight Jacket - A jacket type of garment meant to be worn backwards, consisting of close-ended sleeves that are strapped crisscrossed around the back and tied or locked in place (Houdini used this garment to escape from frequently).

Strap-On - A fastening type strap most commonly used to hold a dildo in place. Commonly used in lesbian sceneing.

Strapping - A length of material, most commonly leather, used for striking the body.

Stretchers - Generally made of wooden dowel rods or metal tubing, having eyelets to secure a submissive's arms and legs apart for play. These are very portable, to use anywhere. Stretchers come in various lengths, usually between twenty four and forty inches.

Subspace - A mental altered state in which a person can be taken to. Space is a form of hypnotism that can be self attained, or a dominant can aid to obtain. Subspace is used for sexual pleasure, and can be used to convert pain to pleasure. After care is mandatory, as is constant monitoring. Not for the novice.

Submissive - One who gives freely of themselves for the pleasures of another. A subordinate with negotiated limits.

Suspension - An advanced form of bondage in which the whole body is suspended off the ground and hanging free.

Note: Not for the novice, use of properly designed equipment is advised.

Swapping - The swapping of one's partner generally for sexual/erotic play. Switching partners temporarily for play purposes.

Switch - One who switches between dominant/submissive roles, from scene-to-scene or within a scene. Some switches may submit to one dominant, and dominate others, etc.

T

Table Play - A padded table where the submissive is restrained for play. The table has many securing points to offer different positions for play or examination. Tables can be used as racks if outfitted accordingly.

Tampon Training - Tampons inserted into the rectum, used as an anal plug for play or punishment.

Tattoo - A permanent form of scarring to the body in the form of various types of pictures or drawings or names, etc. A permanent form of marking the submissive as property.

Teasing - The act of teasing to enhance erotic play or pleasure. Teasing the partner in such a way as to stimulate sexual pleasure.

TENS Unit - Term meaning Transcutaneous

Electrical Neural Stimulation unit. A machine designed to apply electrical impulses to the body at safe levels.

Note: As with any type of electrical play, safety precautions should be observed as this form of play is very dangerous.

Thigh Cuffs - A simple belt around the waist with connectors around it to restrict the submissive's movement of arms and legs.

Thumb Cuffs - Restraining devices used for restraint by the thumbs.

Ticklers - These are sixteen to eighteen inch rods with a tiny flogger attached on the end. Great for small areas where precision impacts are desired. Other ticklers include feathers, sandpaper, etc.

Tickling - Tickling the body to induce laughter. Often used in age play scenes.

Trainer - A dominant who helps submissives understand the sexual aspects of the lifestyle. Study and play sessions are the normal negotiations.

Triple Penetration - Penetration of the body in three bodily orifices.

Example: Insertion of the penis, dildo, butt plug in a female submissive all at once to enhance sexual stimulation.

U

Uniform - Play which involves the submissive wearing a uniform. Such uniforms could include a cheerleader uniform, maid uniform, etc. Commonly used in role-playing scenes.

Urethral Play - Play involving the urethra, the tube that runs between the bladder and the outside of the body. In men it emerges at the end of the penis, and in women near the vagina. Note: Serious damage can occur by inserting inappropriate devices, using excessive force or by bad technique. This form of play is extremely dangerous. Not for the novice.

V

Vibrator - A dildo type device made in varying shapes and sizes and powered by either battery or plug-in electrical type. Used as a form of genital stimulation most commonly for women to promote orgasm.

Violet Wand - A device used commonly in electrical type play which discharges radio energy when touching the body produces electrical sparks. The sensation is similar to static cling charges. Using electricity in BDSM play seems a scary notion to most people, but it can easily be made safe provided two simple rules are followed: only use devices powered by low-voltage batteries and certainly no main-power appliances, avoid placing any contacts above the waist (including the hands or arms) as even small currents in the heart or brain can disrupt those organs' delicate electrical activity with serious consequences.

This form of play is dangerous and not for the novice.

Videos - Pre-recorded movies of a sexual nature.

Can be watching others or being recorded.

Voyeurism - Term meaning the act of watching/peeping. In BDSM play, means to watch someone engage in sex or other forms of sensual/erotic play.

W

Water Torture - A form of torture involving water. After care is extremely important. Example: Laying the submissive face up while dripping water on the forehead for extended periods of time. Derived from the Chinese Water Torture.

Waxing - Using warmed wax as a form of erotic sensation. Common areas of waxing are the buttocks, breast area, back, etc. The process of using hot wax in sceneing.

Weights - Used to extend or pull by pressure. Vaginal weights used on labia, for example, pull the labia to stretch for play or punishment depending on the amount of weight used.

Whipping - A device consisting of a long, flexible striking surface. Whipping the body with a whip type device as a form of punishment.

Whipping Post - Designs vary according to builder, but the principle is to have a tall post with tethers that hang down to attach a person from their wrists. Used for positioning a submissive for ease of whipping. Some dominants use the whipping post for punishment only, and never for play.